WITCH'S RUIN

LADY WITCH SERIES 4

MELISSA MITCHELL

ASIN (eBook): B0CFHN26SB

Cover Art by Jeanine Croft

First Edition, 2023

1 2 3 4 5 6 7

authormelissamitchell.com

For Ania, for listening patiently to me hash out this plot in excited squeals and leading me towards an unexpected ending.

CHAPTER 1

MINA

The wilderness of Raeria was a desolate place, with few travelers brave enough to strike out on their own. One could go days without seeing another face, making it quite lonely, unless of course, your traveling companion was Rixon Kozma. Or, *Prince Aleksander Rixon Kozma*, heir to the Raeriain throne, to be precise. Then you were guaranteed a silent, solid presence by your side, ready to wield a blade at the first sight of gnarled, black skin, or sharp, gnashing teeth.

Demons had made our country this way, sending Raeria's inhabitants cowering behind the safety of towering Nebrine walls. Cut off from friends and family. Relying on the brave souls of trading caravans to bring much needed supplies.

Crack!

A book snapped closed. My charcoal pencil skidded, putting a dark line across my sketch. Rixon considered finishing a book this big, monumental thing; it was his way of applauding. I lifted my gaze, pinning my wielder with a glare, ignoring the small frown on his lips. "Finished it, have you?" He merely grunted. "Well? Was it indeed Carrick?"

"Not even close," he grumbled. "It was Maybell Warren. The healer."

I burst into laughter, far too pleased with myself. "You're awful, you know that? I *told* you she was more suspicious. But *noooo*, you wouldn't—"

"Enough, Lady Witch," he barked, throwing me an affectionate look that didn't match his exasperation. "I understand that despite my prolific reading, I still get duped."

I grinned—couldn't help it. "It's a good thing, no? Think of how boring your mysteries would be if you always managed to guess the culprit."

"I guess them correctly plenty," he grumbled, turning away, letting his gaze dart around the landscape that spread out and away from our lonely road.

"Uh-huh. Well then, how *boring*. You might have to switch to romances instead. Heaven forbid! I'd be happy to loan you a few of mine?"

He scoffed, rummaging in his saddlepack as he tucked the book away. It was his last. But our journey was nearly at an end.

Twelve days in the wilderness, with a few scattered nights spent sleeping in an actual bed. We were closing in on the capital, Corinna. I glanced down at my sketch—a rendition of the winged demon haunting my dreams—stowed the pencil, and closed my journal, wrapping the ties tight before putting it away. My hands were suddenly too shaky to continue anyway. Just the mere thought of our arrival left my mouth dry.

A quick glance at Rixon showed him sitting rigid, his watchful gaze in constant motion. We'd grown lax during our journey. In the past, he never would've spent time in the saddle reading. But my abilities to sense demons had grown, and there hadn't been a single unexpected surprise. He'd taken to reading several times a day, the same way I resorted to sketching. It made our time move faster. It also kept his mind off our destination.

A loud exhale made me glance at him again. I urged Jarrow closer, guiding him with my reins, even though my horse seemed to read my mind. He was an Akeron, a rare but prized breed. Frighteningly fast, perfectly built for strength, speed, endurance, and just plain beautiful with his sleek, black coat. I had known him since he'd breathed his first breath, and dreaded the day when he would breathe his last.

"Are you all right?" I asked Rixon, my voice low, all the teasing bite gone.

He looked at me, expression blank. "Fine, Lady Witch, as I was the last time you asked, and the time before that."

Lady Witch. He still used my title frequently, both in public and private. But only he could say it with a tone that was equal parts respect and affection. An endearment.

"Rix..."

He said nothing. I pressed my lips together, trying to ignore the guilt needling my insides. In the weeks after we'd closed the rift outside Rockfall, he'd been so different. Still on the quiet side, certainly, but far more talkative. That changed the moment I received our new assignment. He'd retreated into himself, uprooting the groundwork I had laid.

"We'll make this quick," I promised him now. "We'll do what we need to do, and get out. I don't want either of us in your father's grasp longer than necessary."

His jaw ticked "Of course."

"I'm serious, Rix. Your father cannot have you."

"As you say, Lady Witch."

I withheld my scoff. "I...I need you to trust me in this, Rixon."

There was a long silence and then, "I do, Mina."

My shoulders relaxed, but not entirely. I knew exactly how he felt about this. There hadn't been much choice, really. The Citadel had sent our next assignment after hearing of our success. The details surrounding how the rift had gotten there were nebulous enough; I certainly had my suspicions. At least in closing it, the number of demons plaguing the kingdom had decreased. They were no longer spilling out of the tear in the earth like a ruptured sore.

And yet, I couldn't help the uncomfortable itch in my chest, that Rixon blamed me for what we were about to endure. That he blamed me for bringing him back to the one place he'd avoided for nearly two decades. The *one* place he'd promised to steer clear of.

I knew how much he was dreading this.

Still, I was forcing him into close proximity with a man who'd physically abused him as a child. A man he hated. A man still intent on snaring him with a birthright he didn't want.

King Maddox Kozma.

I suspected the reason for this assignment—we both did. But I couldn't disobey it, either. I was a witch of the Citadel. Independent as I was, I went where I was bid.

The smudge of the city materialized on the horizon like an ink blot, spreading across parchment the closer we got. We were, perhaps, half a day out when we began passing travelers in small bands. Many nodded politely, some greeting, "Lady Witch," as they passed, others looking at me with suspicion.

At the first narrowed glance, I disregarded it. At the second, I frowned. At the third, I started to itch. It was probably nothing. I focused on the destination ahead.

The edge of the horizon met the sea, where ships traveled freely, keeping Raeria's most prosperous city alive, despite the kingdom's strangled land trade. The road dipped and then rose, taking us to a better vantage point. It was here Rixon pulled Ferrah to a stop. I navigated Jarrow up beside him, giving my horse an affectionate rub. Jarrow was the only thing I had left from my past life—the life I'd run from before settling in at the Citadel—besides my journal, a gift from my mother. Now, its pages were nearly filled.

Rixon's face was blank, unreadable. But there was something in his eyes, a darkness I didn't like. His fist clenched hard on the reins, while his other hand rested atop his thigh, elbow jutting. "This *fucking* place," he muttered, almost too quietly to be heard.

My stomach flopped. I wanted to reach out and touch his arm, to reassure him. What right did I have? I could only pretend to understand what he was going through.

I inhaled and said, "Chin up, Lord Wielder. We've got a job to do."

His nod was distracted.

I clucked and spurred Jarrow down the road, not waiting for him to follow. He would, when he was ready. Judging by the silent minutes that followed, minutes I strained to hear the clip of Ferrah's hooves, he'd needed those minutes.

We passed through farmland, crops arranged in tidy rows, several orchards off in the distance. I blinked, taking in the number of occupied farmhouses, even if I'd sensed the wards we'd passed, miles back—the strongest wards I'd ever felt. Past witches had added to them over the years.

How many were stationed here? I searched through my memory, but came up empty. Perhaps, between five and ten, given the city's size. And yet, they needed me? To do what? Determine the source of a supposed demon outbreak?

As I glanced around, farmers worked, tending to their crops as if nothing were amiss. I didn't see evidence of demons, or an outbreak. Except, something flapped in my chest, a restless recognition.

In the distance, Nebrine walls took shape. My gaze focused on the sight. How many people lived safely behind them? We'd traveled through forts and outposts, but the capital was a city unlike any other. There'd be thousands. Tens of thousands. Even from a distance, it looked double the size of the Citadel. Triple, perhaps?

I inhaled, long and slow, settling myself. The king wanted us here. He'd made these arrangements with the Citadel. Whatever knowledge he'd gotten from his precious general back in Rockfall, he'd found a way to manipulate the Citadel into sending his son back.

I could only wonder what I'd face when we met him. I rubbed Jarrow's neck, cooing at him, telling him what a good boy he was for getting me here safely. He snickered.

How hard could it be, really? Facing Raeria's king? I'd closed an entire rift, killing hundreds of demons. Aside from the one that got away—the one I'd been sketching earlier. If I could manage that, a king shouldn't be a problem, even one as awful as Rixon's father.

So...why did I feel a hard knot growing in my belly, the closer we drew to the city? Like we were approaching a monumental turn in the bend of life? Like whatever happened next, things wouldn't go back to how they were yesterday, or the day before. Something was going to give. My power needed to be ready for it.

⸻

The walls loomed over us, pressing in against me. I drew up my hood, shadowing my features. While I'd grown better at controlling my emotions, my demonic traits were unpredictable.

We came to a stop at the city's portcullis. I tried not to grit my teeth at the discomfort of it. Setting sunlight reflected off the Nebrine walls. A small line of people shifted from foot to foot, waiting to get in—a sight I'd never seen. Most were farmers coming in from a day of work. They produced papers, each one of them, before passing through the walls.

I'd never been forced to wait for entrance into a settlement. I threw Rixon an uneasy look, trying to read him, to glean something about our situation. Was this normal?

He sat silent beside me, a hulking presence. His glower was out in full force, directed towards everything in his path. It was the kind of glare that made others shy away—something he'd mastered years ago.

My mind skidded to a halt. The composure I'd maintained cracked slightly, then entirely. For a brief moment, I saw our situation with absolute clarity. A flush crept over my skin. Oh, *gods*. This was going to be a nightmare—this entire excursion into Corinna.

No. I pushed my misgivings aside. I had every right to be confident. I'd done things other witches could only dream of. It was with that confidence that I straightened my shoulders as we finally, *finally*, reached the front of the line.

"What business do you have in the capital?" A guard stepped forward, flanked by two others. He was mostly unremarkable. On the taller side, brown hair, with a tightly trimmed beard.

I frowned. "We are on assignment. I'm here to meet with your king." I removed my glove, lifting my hand, showing off the markings that labeled me a witch.

The guard's eyes traveled over me, overly slow, before he said, "Ain't heard nothing about a new witch. What could His Majesty need another one for?" He traded a smug glance with the other guards. "Already got six and they ain't doing their jobs."

"Well, I don't suppose *His Majesty* keeps you abreast of his every decision," I snapped, losing patience. "Let us through."

"Hmm..." The guard frowned. "Been strange things happening in the city. Been commanded to be extra careful. Suppose we ought to send word to the palace first, make sure you're expected."

"This is ridiculous," I cried, failing to stop the surge overtaking my voice. My fingers flexed, fisting the reins. Never mind that we'd been traveling for days on end. I was tired, hungry, and uninterested in his power play. "I am a Citadel witch, here on Citadel orders. I'm not some *ruffian* looking to make trouble. Now, step aside."

His smirk boiled my blood.

My nostrils flared. How difficult would it be, to reach behind me and remove my blades? To slice that sneering head right off his shoulders. The hungry thought played out before me, everything else fading—

"Can't be too sure these days," the guard said. I wiped the wicked thought clean. "We'll need to make certain. You just sit tight beside the queue there, while we send up a messenger. Shouldn't take but an hour or two, assuming you're permitted to be here, *Lady Witch*."

I bristled.

Behind me, there came a long, heavy sigh. Rixon urged his horse forward, drawing even with me. The guard's eyes settled on him. A look of uncertainty flashed across the male's face, there and gone. Yes, Rixon had that effect on others. He found his courage and said, "Have you something to add, *Lord Wielder*?"

"Step aside." The deadly low command, a mere two words, landed like a blow. It hit the intended target with a force that left me blinking. The two guards in the back exchanged looks.

"You have no authority here, *wielder*." A disrespectful splat of spit hit the ground beside Ferrah's hooves. My jaw ticked, clenched hard as I struggled against the crackling surge of my emotions.

My sole purpose as a witch was to protect the people of Raeria. Rixon and I risked our lives in the wilderness, slaying demons, so that they might live more safely. This was the respect we received in exchange?

Outright scorn?

Fury clawed up the column of my throat. The shadow of my hood kept hidden the thing thriving inside me. I could feel the dark veins, spreading beneath my skin. Feel the writhing thing—

"No authority, you say?" Rixon's voice was sharp as steel. "I am your *prince*. I outrank you. Now open the *fucking* gate."

I sucked in a gasp, my head whipping to the side. For a moment, my world froze at the sound of Rixon's words—at what he'd just revealed. He sat in his saddle with perfect posture, but the fury on his face, the way his muscles were clenched, said enough. Raeria's heir had returned. All who crossed him would suffer the consequences.

CHAPTER 2

RIXON

A vein in Rixon's neck twitched. He'd lost control. It was so unlike him. Then again, what did it matter *now*? It wasn't as if he could hide his identity whilst here.

"Prince?" muttered the two guards standing back as the other said, "You ain't no prince, or I'm the king of Raeria."

Mina, always sharp, pivoted. "Have a little respect," she commanded. "You are speaking to Alexander Rixon Kozma."

He was already jumping off his horse.

The guard staggered backwards, eyes widening. Rixon grabbed him by his uniform, slamming him against the wall. The guard's skull thunked on the stone. The other two gave shouts of surprise.

Uncertainty flashed across the guard's face. "Her words are true," he growled. "I *am* Prince Aleksander Kozma. Now, if I hear one more fucking word out of your mouth, I'm going to smash your nose and rip out your fucking—"

"Rixon! Enough." He froze. "Stand down."

He dropped his hand, stepping back a pace at the sound of Mina's command. "You're lucky she's got me on a tight leash," he said, eyes narrowing.

 "Return to your horse," Mina added, more calmly this time. She hadn't pulled on the bond, hadn't needed to. He followed her orders without a second thought. She could have told him to fall on his own fucking sword and he would have done it—for her, only for her.

"We're going through now," Mina told the guards. "You may attempt to stop us, if you like. But your prince is rather handy with a blade, and I admit, I wouldn't mind seeing you skewered on the end of one after all this trouble."

The guard's mouth opened and closed, but he didn't attempt to stop them. She spared the male a final glance before she urged Jarrow forward. The other two merely gaped. Jarrow trotted past them, tossing his head and offering a snort of disdain. Rixon followed after, keeping his stare pinned on the guards in warning.

They entered the courtyard, turning their horses towards the city beyond.

Mina sighed, turning towards him. "Was that really necessary, Lord Wielder?"

He blinked, memories of this place engulfing him. His breath stagnated in his chest, got stuck. All around him, the buildings pressed in. "I hate this fucking place," he muttered, ignoring her question.

"Lord Wielder!" she snapped, irritation seeping into her voice.

"Careful, Lady Witch, or I'll put that demanding mouth to work sooner rather than later."

Her cheeks flushed, eyes darting down to his lips.

He sighed, relaxing his muscles and said, "It wasn't necessary, no. I did not mean to lose control like that. It's...it's this fucking place. I hate it here." He cleared his throat, taking a deep breath, squaring his shoulders. "Forgive me, Lady Witch. I do not take kindly to disrespect, not when it is towards you. You were right to rein me in."

"Forgiven, of course," she said, keeping pace beside him. She rubbed her chest, eyes growing distant.

He watched the motion. "What's the matter?"

"I..." She blinked, then swung her gaze towards him. She had the most beautiful hazel eyes, but lately, they often tended towards black, usually when she was distraught. It should have been vile, but it was the opposite. He watched as a tinge of darkness crept into them, felt his heart kick up a notch. "There's something here. Something...demonic. I didn't feel it much until we passed through the walls."

The hairs on the back of his neck prickled. "Then...my father wasn't tricking us?"

"I don't know, Rix. I..." She closed her mouth and frowned, glancing about. He was usually watchful, but was purposefully avoiding it, mostly because he couldn't bear to look at the city that felt like a prison. Cities were considered safe, free of demons, but he had more than demons to worry about now that he was back.

He knew his father, knew what Maddox Kozma was capable of. His father would *kill* Mina if he got the chance. The general's pathetic attempt at assassination was child's play.

Grinding his teeth, he forced himself to look upon the city he'd abandoned. Forced himself to take in the familiar construction of the houses, stacked two and three stories high. Forced himself to look upon the people that would someday be *his* people.

Acid climbed up his throat.

He knew what Mina didn't. His father always won the games he played. She might be powerful, but his father had decades of carefully honed cunning, and an entire kingdom at his command. He rubbed the back of his neck, swearing under his breath. He'd always known, in the end. He'd always known there would be no escaping his father.

"I've never seen a people so unenthused about witches," Mina murmured, keeping her voice low. He was pulled from his dark thoughts. "It's like they were mocking me at the gates. What's...what's going on here, Rix?"

His lips pressed into a tight line. She was right. Aside from noticing their hurried nature—everyone rushing to get indoors, which was also odd—their hostile gazes were hardly welcoming. A few even hissed—fucking *hissed* at her.

He rubbed his tongue along the roof of his mouth, thinking. This had his father's fingerprints all over it. The game, it seemed, had already begun. The king had already poisoned his city against Mina. Against—

A scream ripped through the air, sending chills down his arms. Mina froze, eyes going wide. Around them, those on the street shrieked then disappeared, slamming doors behind them, clicking latches into place. Mina's head whipped around to look at him. He didn't like what he saw written on her face. Without a word, she spurred Jarrow off the street, down a wide alley between buildings.

With the sunlight fading to dusk, the shadows around them stretched and morphed. Mina bounded off Jarrow's back, hands already in motion, her knives pulled free. He was on her heels.

What he saw made him falter. "What the *fuck*?!" he hissed, his stomach twisting. Against the wall, two demons ripped into the flesh of a human—what was left of one—as the mangled body gurgled and then fell silent.

His blade was drawn before he registered the motion. Between him and Mina, the creatures' heads were sliced clean, bodies crumpling to the ground. The human, now a gory heap, was unrecognizable. Mina swore, wiping and stowing her blades out of sight before kneeling, hovering her hands over what was left. He cleaned his blade on a rag from Ferrah's saddlebags, then put it away.

"Dead," Mina concluded. "I cannot save them." She surged to her feet, fists clenched at her sides, looking over the mess of blood and gore, some of it smeared on the brick wall. It looked like dark splotches in the muted light. The stench of iron and demon, like putrid filth, surrounded them.

Mina's throat bobbed, bobbed again. He felt as speechless and shocked as she seemed to be. "I...I don't understand," she managed at last, eyes darting about the alley.

He huffed. Neither did he.

On cue, several warning bells rang out through the city. His head tilted, listening. "Curfew bells, Lady Witch." He knew every message beacon, even if it had been nearly two decades. "We have no way of identifying the body. No one else will be able to, either," he added, keeping his voice low. "Burn what's left."

She gave a shaky nod, making quick work of it. "I felt them," she whispered, turning her wide eyes on him. "I...I can *feel* it, Rixon. Something here." A shiver raced down his spine, a scrape of claws. Her hand went to her chest again, rubbing.

His eyes lingered on the motion.

"It's been a long day, Lady Witch. The sooner I get you settled, the sooner I can breathe again. We can get this sorted after a hot bath."

"Right. Of course." She turned, her arms hugging her stomach as she curled in on herself.

He stepped forward, pulling her against him, wrapping her up. His cheek found the top of her head. She relaxed against him. A few seconds passed before he tilted her face up and kissed her forehead. She relaxed further, the blacks of her eyes returning to normal. He nodded towards Jarrow, then took her waist and lifted her into his saddle. She barked in protest. It always riled her when he did this; he didn't care.

He swung into Ferrah's saddle and led them from the alley. They didn't pass a single person. Everyone was tucked away behind walls, their windows glowing with light, spilling out and casting bright spots along their path.

Five minutes later, the palace loomed before them, its Nebrine-laced walls towering some twenty feet above them, doing little to hide the monstrous edifice jutting up behind it, with its turrets and spires.

His stomach quivered. He took a deep, deep breath. He'd always hoped he would never see it again.

"Halt," a guard ordered, stepping forward.

Even in the glow of torches, he recognized the grizzled face. The man was positively ancient now. The last two decades hadn't been kind. "Hampton?"

Hampton's eyes widened. "Your...Your Highness?" he all but gasped, bowing. "And...and..." His eyes darted towards Mina.

"You may address her as *Lady Witch*," Rixon said, keeping his tone polite.

"Of course. Lady Witch." Hampton's tone was neutral, lacking the mockery he'd heard from the others at the gate. The guard's gaze darted between them. "Heard a rumor you might be back soon. Didn't...wasn't sure it was true. Things been pretty bad, Your Highness."

"I assume my quarters are still kept?"

"Oh. Of...of course." Hampton was already leading them through the palace gate. Inside the main courtyard, Hampton motioned and a young man rushed forward. "Take their horses to the stables, lad. See that they're cared for proper."

Mina dismounted. "Actually, I'll see to my own horse. Rix?"

Rixon nodded. "We'll manage the horses, Hampton. I remember the way."

Hampton looked as if he might protest; his mouth opened, then snapped shut.

"Inform my father that I have returned." The order was redundant. In the next five minutes, the entire palace would know. But it would give Hampton something to do, to feel important. Hampton nodded and rushed away.

He took Ferrah's reins and led her across the courtyard, Mina and Jarrow beside him. The stable hand followed behind them, eyes round, watching. "What's your name, lad?" he asked.

"Al-Aleck Tierney, Your Highness. I...I help with the horses."

He skipped a step, recovering. "Kam Tierney's boy?"

"Aye, sir—Your Highness."

"Last I saw you, you were a wee toddler in diapers, drooling all over the place." Even in the darkness, the dark flush on the lad's face was obvious. Mina's low chuckle met his ears. "What's your father up to these days, Aleck?"

"He...well, just the same as always, Your Highness. The horses." Rixon gave a curt nod as Aleck rushed forward to slide the stable doors open. They rolled on well-oiled wheels.

The king's private stable was a sight to behold. It might not have been extensive, not like the Citadel's, but what the building lacked in size, it made up for in opulence with rich wood, beautiful lanterns, vaulted ceilings, and more. No horse in all the kingdom had a better place to live than here.

"Got a couple empty stalls, Your Highness...Lady Witch." Aleck jogged over to two nearby stalls, side by side, fussing with the latches.

Rixon's gaze fell upon Mina, lingering over her expression of wonder. She'd come to a full stop, lips parted, taking everything in. "It's..." Her eyes snagged on the vaulted ceilings, with large arched beams, before falling to the intricately carved woodwork pillars along the aisles. Hay bales were tidily tucked into alcoves, along with feed barrels, water troughs, a tack wall, saddles...everything. It was a dream—one reflected in her expression and wide eyes.

Horse heads jutted from several stalls, snickering, observing the disturbance of their coming, perhaps getting a good look at their new stablemates. He couldn't help the small smile pulling at his lips. This was, perhaps the one place in all of Corinna, he didn't hate.

A chuckle rose in his throat. "Why do I get the feeling I'll never get you out of here?" he asked, his voice low. Even surrounded by grandeur, it was hard to look anywhere but her. He clenched his fist to keep from reaching for her. To keep from pulling this wondrous woman into his arms—

"Da!" Aleck shouted. "Da, guess who I found!"

He led Ferrah to the empty stall, leading her inside as Kam came around the corner from his office. Their eyes met. It was as if the last fifteen years had never happened. The stalls shrank away until it was just the two of them.

"Well, I'll be!" Kam said, breathless. He strode forward, his movements stilted, forcing Rixon's eyes down.

"You lost your damned leg?!" Rixon growled, right as the old male hooked a hand around Rixon's neck and pulled him in for a hard embrace, thumping him on the back.

"I'd ask what the fuck—" Kam's eyes darted towards Mina and his face turned red. "—*hell* you're doing back here, Aleksander, but I think I already know the answer."

Rixon couldn't pull his eyes from the peg holding the weight of Kam's right leg. His pant leg had been rolled up to the knee.

"Oh, that." Kam waved a hand. "Got trampled by a crazed horse some ten years back. Doesn't much pain me like it used to. Now, boy, you going to introduce me to your lady, or did you lose all your manners the moment you left the palace?"

Rixon snorted. Gods, he'd forgotten how much he liked this stubborn male. "Kam, this is my lady witch, Mina. Mina, this is Kam."

Kam no longer saw her, though. His eyes had fallen on Jarrow and widened. "That's...that's an Akeron—that is. Finest I ever seen. He'll give the king's horses a run, I wager."

"It's a pleasure to meet you, Kam," Mina said, chuckling as she stepped forward. She extended a hand, her markings visible. Kam ripped his gaze from Jarrow and took it, kissing her knuckles, eyes twinkling. Then he pinned Rixon with a knowing stare. "Wondered what could keep you away for so long. Should have known it'd be a beautiful female."

Mina cleared her throat, glancing between them. "I take it there's history here? " Her eager expression was all too obvious. A smile stretched across her lips.

Rixon shifted as his guilt got the better of him. During their journey here, she asked for stories of his childhood. He'd refused, despite knowing how eager she was for knowledge of his past.

Here she stood, face bright, fishing. An ache formed in the back of his throat. He'd been such an asshole. The last thing he wanted was a repeat of history, for his past to come between them.

He needed to do better.

"Didn't bother to mention me, eh, Aleksander?" Kam's attempt to scold fell flat. "Well then..."

"Nothing personal, old man." He reached over and squeezed Kam's shoulder before turning to Mina. "Kam has known me since I was in diapers," he explained, searching for forgiveness in her expression. "He taught me to ride. He's the reason I care for horses the way I do."

"Oh, come now. Don't go all sentimental on me, boy."

"He also never told my father whenever I hid away in the stable."

"Well, that was awfully kind of you, wasn't it?" Mina said, a soft expression washing over her features. Kam merely grunted.

Rixon turned back to the stable master. "Not sure how long we'll be here, but at least our horses will be in good hands."

"The best," Aleck said, proudly lifting his chin.

"I take it he's finicky?" Kam asked, motioning towards Jarrow. "May I meet him?"

"Oh, yes." Mina clucked and pulled on the reins, urging Jarrow forward. The horse regarded Kam and Aleck with wary eyes.

Kam took a single step forward, producing an apple from his pocket, which immediately got Jarrow's attention. Mina let out a breathy laugh, one that had Rixon's stomach tightening. He loved that sound from her.

"You're a fine fellow, aren't you?" Kam said.

"*Tuo roka, Jarrow. Ero ah nineen.*" Mina's murmur was low, but loud enough. Jarrow's ears pricked. *You're okay*, she'd said. *He's a friend*.

"Well, I'll be damned," Kam said. Then, "*Hinnin, lekke roy.*" Jarrow's ears pricked at that, and the horse took a tentative step forward, before lowering his head and snatching the apple from Kam's hand, then stepping back to the safety of Mina's body.

"You speak Aavix," Mina observed.

"Aye, Lady Witch."

"Good." She nodded, pleased.

"Let's get them settled," Kam said, as Jarrow lowered to snatch up the last portion of apple that had fallen from his mouth.

They made quick work of the task. He used the time to ask Kam about what was happening in the city—telling him what they'd seen on their way in. The question made Kim stiffen. "It's been getting worse the past couple weeks," Kam informed them.

Mina was busy brushing Jarrow, she paused to listen.

"At first," Kam continued, "it only happened once or twice, and no one quite believed it was demons that done it. After all, demons inside a city? Unheard of. Can't get in through the Nebrine walls—supposedly."

"How often, now?" Rixon asked, keeping his voice low in case anyone happened to step into the stables.

"Daily, sometimes. I keep Al close by—don't let him out into the city at night. He knows better than to leave the palace walls unless necessary."

"Only at night then?"

"Mostly. There been a few during the day, but night seems more frequent. Your father's been blaming the witches. Says they ain't doing their job."

Rixon stilled. Interesting, very interesting. He and Mina shared a furtive glance.

"Something tells me that ain't the case?" Kam asked. "Reckon you're here to sort everything out?"

"Something like that," Mina said, wiping her hands, stepping away from Jarrow.

"Well, be careful, the both of you. King Maddox likes his games, and you know how he feels about you, boy."

Rixon nodded.

"Either of you need anything—anything at all, and you let me know."

"Thank you, Kam," Mina said, reaching for one of his grizzled hands, taking it in both of hers and shaking it warmly.

"Know it ain't his job, but I'll send Al up to check on you both periodically."

Rixon took hold of Kam's shoulder, giving it a squeeze, before grabbing their saddlebags, hoisting them over his shoulder, and leading Mina out of the stables. He could no longer put off what he'd been dreading. It was time to face the life he'd run from.

CHAPTER 3

MINA

Being in the stables eased a measure of my tension, but not enough. I could sense the ominous press of demons, an itching pressure against my chest. Not to mention whatever was going on between Rixon and I.

Kam was an easy presence, paired with the smell of hay, and Aleck's excited eyes when he'd seen Jarrow, and my mood *was* improved. I always turned into a hopeless ball of goo when someone admired my horse. Knowing Jarrow was well cared for gave me one less thing to worry about.

We were silent as we strode through the palace. I opened my mouth several times—to ask about an archway, or a fountain, or a statue—only to think better of it. Rixon didn't want to discuss his childhood. He'd made that clear. I didn't fault him for it. I tried not to take it personally, despite the heaviness in my chest. He'd talk about it when he was ready. And if he never was? Well, I would need to accept that.

Servants spotted us and either gazed curiously at our passing, or fumbled and gasped, rushing to bow. Rixon had been gone a long time, but those who'd worked here long enough recognized him. A pair of males in black and gold livery rounded the corner, conversing in low voices.

"You there," Rixon said, getting their attention. The pair froze, then immediately dropped into bows. His authoritative voice gave them reason enough, even if they didn't recognize him. His appearance was a little rough around the edges. "Have dinner prepared and brought to my chambers."

"Your...your chambers, my...my...lord?" the taller of the two said.

"*That's* the crown prince, you idiot," the shorter, darker skinned male hissed, elbowing his comrade, whose eyes widened.

"At-at once, Your Highness," they both echoed.

Rixon nodded and set off again. I watched the entire exchange with a frown, then hurried to catch up. I didn't comment on the incident. I distracted myself by taking in my surroundings, noting walkways and corridors, various doors, courtyards, and other features of the king's palace. It reminded me of the Citadel, but grander. Far, far grander. Portions of the corridors were wide, arched hallways, lined with statues of military—knights in armor, soldiers holding spears, and the like. There were elaborate wooden doors leading...who could say where. Other hallways were closed in with glass windows, boasting plush carpeting and displays of art—statues, sculptures, framed landscapes, portraits.

We traversed several sets of stairs until I was hopelessly lost. Rixon ignored everyone we passed, nobles and servants alike. His stride exuded an air of superiority. I found myself stealing glances in his direction. I'd never seen him walk quite like this. Shocking, that there could be any difference, since he was always so confident.

We entered another overly opulent corridor, this one hosting very few doors. I strode along, taking in the dark views from each of the glittering windows, the orange city lights spread below in neat rows and blocks. We were several floors above, and the view by day would be staggering. Between the windows, there were giant bouquets of flowers, each in an elegant vase, resting on pedestals. They were fresh and expertly arranged—

"Here, Lady Witch."

I jumped, glancing beside me. Rixon had stopped somewhere behind me. I spun and found him at a set of double doors, hands clenched on the knobs. Others might not have noticed the whites of his knuckles. I rushed over, feeling my cheeks heat. Had he noticed my distraction—how captivated I'd become?

Rixon turned the knobs and pushed the doors inward. They gave without hesitation, swinging open silently on well oiled hinges. Even with the scarce light, what little spilled inside from the corridor, I could tell it was the grandest suite I'd ever seen. I took a step forward, only to have Rixon's arm snake around my waist, pulling me back against him. "No, Lady Witch. Stay here," he commanded, breath tickling my ear.

My lips parted. I felt my eyes blackening at the command, at the way I craved it. I relaxed against him just before he released me.

Witches of the Citadel were supposed to give the commands. That's how it had always been. I was an exception, because I so desperately enjoyed submitting to him. Even if it was only done in the bedroom, where I willingly gave it all to him.

He strode forward, checking the space, his shadow moving through the darkness. I saw a spark flash before wall sconces blazed to life. Soon, the chamber was glowing.

"It's all right," he said at last, turning towards me. He stood frozen in the center of the room as I entered. I felt his gaze. Gone was the rigid assuredness of his posture, replaced with uncertainty. Vulnerability.

My pulse increased to a rapid staccato. I strode across the room, unsure where to look first, captivated by the opulence. My feet made the decision for me, stopping before a large desk, nearly four feet long. I glanced over the old parchment, yellowed with time. Some of it was arranged neatly in stacks, while other sheets were scattered and disorganized. Inkwells, some still containing ink and others empty, littered the surface. Several quills—a couple broken—and charcoal pencils completed the mess. All of it had been sitting, waiting for his return as if he'd only just left.

I schooled my features, careful not to laugh. He'd always struck me as organized. Certainly, the rest of his suite appeared tidy. But this, the beating heart of the space? This was chaos. I wasn't sure how he'd managed to accomplish a single thing, sitting here in this mess.

I lifted a hand, caressing one of the feathered quills sitting upright in a holder. A sheet of his notes caught my gaze, probably from his lessons as a boy. It was extremely beautiful penmanship, with elegant, slanted lines and perfect loops. I stared at it. I'd never seen his handwriting before. The kind I'd expect from a court pansy, certainly, but not a gruff warrior, so at odds with the state of disarray the desk was in.

I stepped away, absorbing more of the large room. My chest expanded. I'd been given so little of his life before the Citadel. *So little*. It had only made me want more. Now I devoured it like a starved creature.

A giant armoire stood closed. I opened it. Neatly arranged by color, I found an entire wardrobe of royal clothing, lost in time. I grazed my hand over a velvet tunic, tugging it out, then chuckled. This would have fit twelve-year-old Rixon, certainly not the thirty year old male now dominating the room.

Another cabinet revealed weapons, smaller than those he used now. Some were obviously for training. There were other trinkets too, for mathematics, astronomy, and the like—tools for learning. Near the cabinet was a set of bookshelves. My gaze flicked over it, over the hundreds of books arranged within. He'd been a reader, even in his younger years. A small smile pulled at the corner of my mouth.

A vision swam before my eyes. I could see him here as a young boy, nestled on the sofa, book in hand. The frown that sometimes drew a line between his brows, out in full force.

I moved on, studying everything else. Sitting room furniture had been covered over with white sheets to keep the dust at bay. I began uncovering everything, peeling back the skin to review

the thing beneath. Rich, plush sofas and chaise lounges uphol-
stered with dusty blue and gold fabric, accented with end tables
and vases, all centered around a large, white and gray marble
fireplace. Atop the mantle were animal figurines made of solid
gold.

A dining table of rich brown wood sat in its own alcove near
the large, floor to ceiling windows. It seated six. When I peered
through the glass, I found a private torchlit garden below,
glowing in the darkness. There were paths winding through it,
and a tall wall surrounding it.

It was utterly *enchanting*! My insides warmed. I wanted to go
down to it, to explore it. Instead, my gaze lingered a beat longer
before I turned away. Opposite the sitting room, through a set
of sliding wooden doors, was the sleeping area, with a matching
bed and canopy, set up on a platform. I pulled the coverings off
the bedspread, revealing fabric that matched the furniture.

Through a side door, I found a bathing room and toilet, with a
sunken tub nearly the size of a pool. *Gods*! He'd been a spoiled
brat, hadn't he?! But I loved him despite it. I was already
desperate to draw water and collapse into it. My gaze swallowed
up the elaborate tile, also pale blue, with gold filigree worked
in, before emerging and shutting the door behind me.

The entire suite was as large as the home I'd grown up in.

A sight on the bedside table caught my eye. I strode over to it.
A stuffed bear missing one of its button eyes. The poor thing
looked as if I touched it, it might fall apart. I caressed the old
teddy with the point of my index finger. It was a childhood
item, well loved. He'd been in his adolescent years when he'd

run away—too old for such things by then. Had it sat here even after he'd outgrown it?

The thought of *my wielder*, tall and opposing—a man who could swipe the head off a demon in seconds—keeping a teddy on his bedside table, was enough to undo me. "I never took you for the stuffed bear type," I cooed, hiding my warm affection behind teasing words.

Rixon simply stood there, muscles tense, watching with wary eyes. "Are you quite done, Lady Witch?" A slight flush crept up his neck, but his exasperated tone only spurred me on.

"And all those books on your shelves, I can only imagine how you'd hide away reading. That explains your silent nature, I suppose. We'll have to throw out all the clothes in the wardrobe, since they won't fit you anymore." I fought off a smile threatening to break free. "And by the way, your desk is *deplorable*. But at least your penmanship is adequate."

Adequate. It was so far beyond that. Still, I said it knowing full well it was the most beautiful penmanship I'd ever seen.

He made a noise in the back of his throat, stalking across the room, grabbing me by the waist and burying his face in my neck, scratching his stubble over my skin as he began nipping. Laughter broke free of my chest. "Insufferable, *insufferable* female," he growled.

My laughter grew louder, but died immediately as he shoved his fingers into my hair, taking hold of me, pulling my head back and claiming my mouth. Mirth was replaced with heat. This. *This* was the Rixon I was familiar with. Passionate, worshipful, loving.

He hardened against my stomach, his erection growing. Sensation curled deep in my core, making my body ache. I was too ready for him.

He kissed me harder, his wet tongue roving against mine, exploring. A tiny noise rose from the depths of my throat. All my earlier worries disappeared. I wasn't thinking about the demons within city walls. I wasn't thinking about how commanding Rixon had been towards everyone here, or how easy he'd stepped back into the role. I wasn't ruminating over his closed offness, unwilling to share his past. I wasn't thinking about much of anything, really, besides the growing ache between my legs, the wetness of his mouth, the liquid pooling at my apex.

In this moment, there was only the cage of his body around mine.

He groaned, deep, low, and I knew that sound, recognized it. His control was slipping. He deepened our kiss until we were clawing at each other, our breaths heavy and mingled, me trying to find purchase as I grasped his muscled shoulders, his neck, his face, his hair. Him as he pulled against my waist, my hips, pressing our groins together, grinding his length against me, melding my chest to his. My nipples hardened against him—

A throat cleared.

I froze, my body turning rigid. Rixon didn't bother pulling back. I tried to push away but his grip was iron. He simply slowed his efforts, then sweetly ended our kiss, nipping at my lower lip, his breath hot against my skin. Blood rushed to my cheeks. We'd left the door *wide* open. Now the entire palace would know just how *entangled* we were.

Rixon didn't bother releasing me. He wouldn't, not now, not with his cock tenting in his pants. He simply angled his head towards the entryway, glaring. A servant stood, bearing a tray laden with food, his mouth gaping, eyes darting between us.

"Put it on the table," Rixon commanded, his voice firm but lacking any bite. Another servant scuttled in behind, carrying a pitcher and cups. My wielder straightened slightly and said, "What are your names?"

The one with the tray set it down, rushing to attention. "Ansel, Your...Your Highness. And—"

"Florian, Your Highness," said the other, setting down the pitcher, fumbling with his fingers until he tucked his hands behind his back.

Rixon gave a tight nod. "See that a liquor cabinet is purchased and stocked for this room. It can go over there." He waved a hand in the general direction. I glanced at the empty span of wall near the bookshelves.

Ansel and Florian exchanged surprised looks. "Tonight—?"

"Tomorrow, obviously. There will be no more disturbances tonight. My lady witch and I have unfinished business." He finally released me, producing a couple coins, handing them over. Both male servants nodded vigorously, their eyes darting downward to the clear evidence on display, Rixon's pants, then scurried away.

I pressed both hands to my mouth, sniffling my laugh. A moment later, the soft click of a door meant we were alone. "I *knew* you were bossy, but—"

Rixon moved. He hoisted me up level with his mouth and attacked it. A squeal left my lips as my legs wrapped about his hips. He marched me towards the door, slamming my back against it none too gently. A predator's smile spread across my lips. I felt the darkness living inside me rise up, blackening my eyes. His lips were on mine again, forcing my mouth wide as his tongue swept in, claiming.

My low groan hardly sounded like me. I squeezed my thighs tight around him, the urge to clamp them together intensifying. My hands lifted, fingers curling, ready to rip his tunic to shreds. I needed his bare chest. Needed *him*.

Instead—

"*Stop*," I commanded, pulling on the bond. He froze. He would have stopped had I simply asked him, but...well, I was in a mood. I let my legs slide down his body, slowly, achingly slowly, so that I rubbed against his hard length. He groaned, his breaths irregular.

"We will continue this shortly. First, I must ward the door. Then you're going to give me a bath, Lord Wielder. After that, we'll have our dinner." My voice was hardly my own, full of needy want and something...darker.

Rixon's pupils blew wide, his eyes growing desperate. "Yes, Lady Witch," he rasped, his chest rising and falling more rapidly.

There was a time when he'd hated, even feared the bond. Now, he positively *craved* my control. Went wild for it. I glanced down, noticed the way his hands strained to reach for me, fists clenching, unclenching. Like a rabid animal pulling on a chain, desperate to break free. Desperate to continue ravaging me.

We were back on common ground. In this, we could meet in the middle, no matter what demons lurked in his past. No matter how strained things might be as a result of coming here. This was the place we came back together. A place where our bodies created the bridge that knit us back together.

A pleased huff fell from my lips. I rose onto my tiptoes, placing my mouth against the shell of his ear. He shuddered at the wisp of my touch. "I love seeing you unhinged, Rixon, darling." Such a soft endearment for such a strong male. "I love seeing you desperate and needy for me. Shall I make you work for it tonight? Shall I force you on your knees?"

"Yes, anything," he rasped. "All of it—whatever you wish. Let me please you."

A low growl of a laugh rumbled up in my chest. I came back down on the flats of my feet. "Hmm...we shall see." I left it at that, left him wondering just what tonight's games might hold. Left him to his imagination as I turned my back on him and began warding the door.

CHAPTER 4

RIXON

Rixon took one gasping breath after another, pushing against the bond restraining him. The pressure in his pants, the ache, was near unbearable. *Damn* this woman of his, for being so fucking irresistible, for driving him mad with need. The moment she released him, he would rip her free of her garments and bury himself deep—

A loud knock scattered his thoughts. Mina froze where she'd been finishing with the wards.

"I explicitly said I was not to be disturbed," he bit out. He tugged again, uselessly. The bond held.

"For...forgive me, Your Highness," came a hesitant voice. Another servant. "His Majesty, the king, has summoned you."

The muscle in his jaw ticked. He took a deep, calming breath. "Well, you can tell His Majesty the king, my *father*, that I intend to see to my lady witch's needs before I attend to him."

A long silence followed. Perhaps the servant had gone— "And how long will that be...Your Highness?"

He growled low in his chest. Couldn't he have one fucking night? Was it too much to ask?

Were he a better male, a stronger male, equipped to stand up against his father, he'd have outright refused. "I do not know. We will proceed once we are settled." There was a time he dropped everything for his father, jumped when summoned, do exactly what was asked. That time was long gone. And yet, he couldn't quite free himself.

"Of course, Your Highness. Of course."

He waited another moment, then exhaled. The leash holding him disappeared, but he didn't move. "Well, so much for our fun tonight," Mina pouted.

He lunged for her, lacing his fingers through her hair, tilting her head, forcing her to look up at him. "We are *hardly* finished, my little witch. I believe you said something about me on my knees? I will happily comply—no need for the bond."

Before she could react, he dropped to his knees and made quick work of the ties holding her pants in place. They were around her knees in seconds as he pushed her against the door, slipping a finger between her lush thighs, sliding it along her slit. He hissed, spreading her wetness up and around her clit. She groaned, going limp against the door, tangling her fingers into his hair. It came free of its tie, thick locks falling around his face.

Holding her gaze, he lifted the wet finger to his mouth and made slow work of licking it clean. Chills spread over his skin

—a response to her eyes as they blackened, dark veins spreading outwards. His heart began to race. Was it fucked up that he enjoyed claiming her like this? Enjoyed how powerful it made him feel? Enjoyed watching her lose control of the thing lurking inside her?

He'd never been one for mild sex, except on the rare occasion that his mood craved love making. Getting her like this felt exotic, addicting. Like he was fucking something that was both Mina, and otherworldly, simultaneously. He would *never* get enough.

"Rixon," she gasped. He dipped his head and licked at her entrance. Her legs, restrained by the pants around her knees, made things more challenging but didn't stop him. The taste of her drenched his tongue. "Rixon," she said this again, more forcefully.

He hesitated, keeping his nose against the curls at her apex. "Yes, *Lady Witch*?" She shivered when his voice coated her skin.

"Take me into the bath before you get too carried away." A question more than a demand, despite the darkness riding her voice. He stood, scooping her up, carrying her to the bathing chamber where he drew a bath. As the sunken tub filled, he removed the remainder of her clothes, then began on his.

They didn't discuss his father's request. Didn't tarnish their heated moments with the thought of him. For that, he was grateful, so fucking grateful. His father could wait an eternity, for all he cared. The only thing that mattered was Mina's needs. Let the king stew while he fucked his lady witch, while he buried his cock deep, feeding her pleasure—

"No, let me," Mina said, wrapping her fingers around wrists while he fussed with his tunic. "I want to do it."

"As you wish," he managed, letting his arms drop. She'd gotten more and more fussy with him. More possessive. It should have irritated him. Instead, he felt cherished, adored.

His tunic fell to the floor. She began messing with the ties on his pants. Those too fell. Her gentle fingers caressed his skin, sliding over the rigid lines of muscles on his abdomen. Heat followed each caress, burning. His muscles tightened.

She didn't touch his dick, standing fully erect and ready. She knew how much it riled him when she ignored it. "I could lick every inch of you," she purred, "and never be satisfied."

He chuckled low. "Such a bold declaration, Mina, but I'll be doing the licking tonight."

She glanced up at him, the blackness in her face gone, replaced with a shy, soft smile. Those had grown rarer, as she'd grown bolder, more at ease with her sexuality. But he still cherished them, still loved when he could say things that made her shy. Do things that made her blush.

"The bath is full, Mina. Get in before I toss you in. Actually —" He glanced at the tub. "No. Go lay on the side there and open your legs for me like a good little witch." Her breath hitched, eyes darting to the edge of the sunken tub, to the floor where he wanted her to lay. "Don't make me repeat myself."

A low threat rode his words.

He loved the sight of her skin erupting in goosebumps. She dropped her hand from his chest and walked over to the side of the tub, letting her feet dangle in the water. She laid back, lifting her feet to the edge, bending her knees, spreading her thighs wide for him.

His abdomen clenched, the ache in his cock intensifying. "Look at you," he managed, stalking over to the pool of water, taking the stairs as he descended into its hot depths. It came up to his waist. He waded to the other side, planted his hands on the edge, and looked at Mina's flushed face between her parted thighs. Her chest rose and fell, breasts peaked towards the ceiling.

"You are so very beautiful, so fucking perfect," he whispered, taking this moment to worship her existence. Then he buried his face, dragging his nose over her clit, lapping at her cunt, letting her strangled cries guide him. Each one grew more demonic in nature, each one had him clenching. He dropped a hand and wrapped it around his cock, stroking himself, groaning.

"Rix—please," she gasped.

"Yes, little demon?" At his question, she huffed. "Well? What is it you're asking for? Use your words."

"Your fingers. Use your fingers, too. And *stop stroking yourself*, for the gods' sake. I want you needy and desperate for me."

"Is that so?" he growled, a challenge.

"Yes. I forbid it."

His lips parted, but he disguised his surprise. "My, my," he tsked. "Very well then. I'll restrain myself, but just so you know, I'll fuck you harder for making me wait, you difficult little creature."

"Good," she breathed, turning her gaze towards the ceiling. That was all it took. He descended upon her, slipping his fingers in, paired with his tongue, until her body was so tight, her walls fluttering around him. And then he withdrew.

She gave a cry of frustration, but he was already lifting her, dragging her into the pool. Her face was flushed, a mixture of heat and blackened veins. She looked like a vengeful goddess, come to wreak havoc on the world, inky black hair fanning out around them. A chill raked its claws down his spine, heightening his arousal.

She might have been the most powerful witch in Raeria—or even, the world. But she belonged to *him*, and he knew exactly how to control her. Exactly how to bring her to her knees.

There was nothing soft about the way he claimed her, then. The demonic power in her rose up and welcomed it, begged for more as he buried himself with a single thrust. He was still careful with her, wrapping his arms around her back and waist to ensure the lip of the tub didn't bite into her, but that was as much as his gentleness allowed.

Water sloshed out as he fucked her, each thrust earning a heady cry. His balls tightened but he forced himself to last, forced her to last, too. He slowed his movements each time she tightened, approaching her orgasm. He repeated his torture until she was all but sobbing, clinging to him, *begging*.

"Tell me, little witch. Tell me what you are to me," he demanded.

"Yours," she gasped. "Fuck, Rix." Her voice was a hiss. "Yours. Always yours."

"Yes, good girl. And tell me, what might you do to feel my cock buried deep inside of you like this?"

"Anything," she cried. "*Everything*." And then he didn't stop, letting her spasm around him. She milked him with needy drags. A tingle started at the base of his spine, spreading. He roared, his neck straining as he dropped his head into her hair, clamped down on her ear hard enough to send a little, pained scream from her lips. His orgasm ripped through him.

"Yes," she breathed. He groaned, slowing his movements. The aftershocks pressed through him, wave after wave, then slowed to a stop, leaving him numb.

He lifted his head, studying her ear. He hadn't drawn blood, but he'd been, perhaps, too rough. "Did I—are you—?"

"I told you it was fine," she managed between breaths. "I *like* when you're rough. When..."

He lifted a brow, walking them over to the ledge of the tub, sitting down, without leaving the warmth of her cunt. "When, *what*? Say it, Mina."

"When you..." Her throat bobbed. They'd had this conversation more than once, and they'd have it again. It was a way of checking in with her. A way to ensure that he didn't push too far, beyond what she was comfortable with. "When you *hurt* me," she admitted at last.

He gave a rough nod, moving her so that she straddled him, keeping himself planted. "And you'll tell me? You'll stop me if it's too much? Use the bond if you must?"

She sighed, loudly. "No, Rixon. I'm tired of having this conversation." Already, the blackness was receding from her eyes, disappearing until normal skin and hazel irises remained. He inhaled deeply, pressing their chests together, enjoying the feel of her slick nipples against him.

"I don't want to hurt you, Mina. Not—I mean, not in any detrimental way."

"But...you *do* want to hurt me a little bit, don't you?"

His skin heated, enticed by the thought. He clamped down on the emotion, dropping his gaze. "I'm not a bad person, Mina."

"I never said you were, but you *do* want to hurt me, don't you?"

"Stop it," he managed, swallowing.

"Tell me, Rixon. Tell me what you want to do to me?" It wasn't a command. She could have used the bond. Instead, she was letting him choose.

"Fuck, woman." The words came out a loud growl. He hesitated. "I want to take you over my knee and redden your ass every time you talk back with that sassy little mouth."

"Mmm-hmm. Which you've already done more than once."

Yes, and he'd nearly come in his pants, just doing it.

"I want to bite you. Fucking bite you until I see my teeth marks marring your beautiful skin." She hummed in acknowledgement. Gods, he was a fucking masochist, wasn't he? "I want to tie you to my bed with restraints, tight enough to hurt. Tight enough to leave marks."

"Mmm-hmm...and do you want to hit me?"

He stilled, his skin turning to ice. "What?! No," he sputtered. "No, Lady Witch. Never." That's where he drew a line. A *hard* line.

"No kicking, punching?"

His stomach twisted. "Fuck, no. Never that." He ran a hand through his hair, hating where this conversation had gone, the way it twisted his stomach. Made him feel ill.

She nodded, something settling in her expression. "I like the kinds of pain you've proposed. I want to feel it."

"No, Mina—"

"*Yes*, Rixon. You aren't going to truly hurt me. You aren't interested in physically abusing me, not that I'm judging people out there who want to feel something beyond what you've outlined. Rixon..." His eyes darted over her face, fingers tightening around her waist. "I trust you. I know you would never truly hurt me. And even if you draw blood, I heal."

He swallowed. "You don't...you don't think I'm fucked up for getting excited about it? About being overly rough with you?"

"I'm not a delicate thing," she said, then pressed her forehead against his. He exhaled. "I'm... I'm eager to explore these things with you. Everything we've done so far has been..." A shudder worked through her. "Has been *good*. Things I never thought I'd like. Like when you spank me. You've seen what it does to me."

His cock twitched. It was still buried in her. The sensation made him grit his teeth. He couldn't help the reflex, pulling her hips forward a little, groaning. The memory of her ass in the air, her body flipped over his knee while he'd recently spanked her, stinging his palm, feeling how wet she'd grown in the process...

She leaned back to regard him. The memory fractured. She wrapped her fingers around his neck and kissed him. It was soft, loving, reassuring.

"There's nothing wrong with having...exotic tastes, Rix, as long as we discuss them beforehand. You've always been good about that. But don't be shy. Don't hold back, just for fear or embarrassment. Talk to me about it, if...if it's something that arouses you. All right?"

"All right," he croaked, his throat dry. He hadn't expected her to push him like this.

"Now, as much as I want to continue this,"—she wiggled her hips and his center tightened—"and perhaps let you bite me this time, *really* bite me, not just those love bites you like, we need to have dinner and meet your father, no?"

The heat inside him snuffed right out. She rose off his stiff cock and waded over to the soap dish at the edge of the bathing pool. Then she turned to him. "Come, Lord Wielder. I will wash you."

What a cruel, *cruel* female. Still, he stood because he had no choice but to comply.

CHAPTER 5

MINA

We strode through the palace. I dared a glance at Rixon to find his jaw tight. He'd been in a mood, ever since our discussion about sex and pain. It embarrassed him—the desires he held close to his heart. I'd noticed that immediately. A surprise, certainly, since there was little capable of making him flush the way he had in the bath.

"You know where you're going?"

"It's not something easily forgotten, Lady Witch," he said, words clipped. We approached a set of doors flanked by guards. Rixon stopped me with a hand on my shoulder, just out of earshot. "You are my lady witch. I will defer to you. You know this, yes?"

"Of course, Rixon." I frowned at his sudden urgency. "I didn't stop being your lady witch when we walked into the palace."

His eyes darted between mine, but at last, he nodded.

I realized what he meant—why he'd stopped me. Despite acting like a prince, barking orders when it suited him, he was still my wielder, and that took precedence.

"And the thing inside you?" he asked "My father will bait me. Can you control it?"

"I..." My fingers twitched at my sides. I curled them into fists. I couldn't let the king see what I'd become. Taking a confident breath, I gave a single nod. "I can—I will."

"If you have any misgivings, any whatsoever, we can turn around, go back to my room. I can meet with him later."

I pulled my shoulders tight until they ached. "No. We get this over with."

He gave a single nod. "Very well. After you, Lady Witch." He held out a hand, directing me forward. I set off at a confident pace.

"We're here to see the king," I said when we reached the door, Rixon standing slightly behind me.

The guards saluted, but their eyes were on Rixon. "Your Highness," they said in unison.

Rixon ignored them. I cleared my throat. "Are you going to let us through, or shall I open the doors myself?"

Finally, *finally*, their gazes fell upon me. "The king requested his son, Prince Aleksander," one of them dared.

"Well," I said, glancing down to fuss with my sleeve, "I'm afraid we are a package deal. Shall we come back later?" They shifted, uneasy. "*No*? Fine. Open the door."

A hesitant sigh and then, "Of course, Lady Witch." The one on the right reached out and twisted the knob, stepping into the chamber, announcing our arrival. I didn't bother waiting. Why should I? I swept in, walking past the guard and into the middle of the room, Rixon on my heels.

It reminded me of Rixon's in terms of amenities, and yet, everything was twice as large, twice as extravagant. An entire apartment for a king. And standing near the window, looking down into the same garden beneath Rixon's room, stood a man with his back to us.

King Maddox Kozma.

Even from this view, there was something about him, something I couldn't quite put my finger on. Despite the dark thing living in me, it sent chills down my spine. He wasn't...*right*.

"That will be all, Leo. Thank you," said the king. His voice was deep, not so different from my wielder's. The guard, Leo, backed out of the room, shutting the door behind him. I only discerned his retreat in the window's reflection, just as I could see Rixon standing behind me. The king could, too. He watched us where he stood, back facing the room.

"You answered the Citadel's request, I see." His hands were clasped behind him.

"I would hardly call it a request." My voice remained steady. I willed myself to remain calm. A test, one I'd failed the last time, facing his general.

King Maddox Kozma slowly turned to face us. I blinked, blinked again. It was like looking at an older version of Rixon. I had expected similarities, but, *gods*! It was eerie. There were differences, too. His hair was light, where Rixon's was dark. And his body was lithe and toned, where Rixon's was built and powerful.

King Maddox Kozma strode forward, coming to a stop ten paces away. Closer, I noticed his age more clearly, and something else. There was a sickness clinging to him, like the skin over his bones had turned waxen, as if he were merely...*existing*.

Another shiver raced through me.

His eyes fell on Rixon and a muscle near his temple jumped. A tick. His was a long perusal, ending in a slight sneer. I would not have recognized it, subtle as it was, were I not already familiar with Rixon's tells.

The king turned back to me. "Thank you for bringing my son home. You may leave now." He flicked a dismissive hand, turning back to my wielder. "Return to the Citadel or, whatever backwater place you come from."

I snorted. "Believe me, Your Majesty, I would be all too eager, had I not seen there are demons lurking amidst your city streets, but I would be taking Rixon with me."

"Ah. Rixon now, is it? Is *that* what you go by, boy?" The king's gaze remained entirely on my wielder. I bristled but kept myself in check. From the window's reflection, I saw that Rixon gazed back, expression unyielding. He didn't answer.

I sighed, feigning more exasperation than I felt. "Is there a *reason* you summoned us tonight, Your Majesty? We are travel worn. Do make it quick. I'd like to return to my bed."

"I don't recall granting you a bed. It was Aleksander I summoned, not you."

I felt the subtle twitch of Rixon, a signal through the bond.

"Let me make something abundantly clear, *Your Majesty*. Rixon belongs to me."

"He *belongs* to his country."

"Perhaps, once upon a time, but you chased him away."

"I did nothing of—" He stopped himself before falling prey to my taunts. "I am not having this conversation with you. This is how things will go. You have the evening to bid your wielder goodbye. On the morrow, you will depart."

"Or what?"

"Or you will wish you had."

I took a step forward. "No, Your Majesty, *this* is how things will go. We will stay and complete our assignment, and *you* will explain why there are demons within your city walls." This time, I allowed a sliver of black to seep into my gaze, just a flash of it—there and gone.

King Kozma's gaze darted over my face. He was good, so very good, at hiding his surprise. Only a single blink. But he'd seen it.

There'd be time later to consider the move. Whether it scared him, or simply sealed my doom. It was naive to think the general hadn't already mentioned what he'd seen from me, but if he hadn't, secrecy was my own card to play.

"Now." I smiled. "Explain."

He gave a dismissive shrug, as if admitting defeat, or rather, pretending to. He'd known I wouldn't give up easily. Just as the general had known his attempt to kill me wouldn't be successful. But he'd needed to try, after all.

I doubted his future attempts would be so straightforward, especially with his not-so-subtle threat. It if was a game of cat and mouse he wanted, fine. I was up for the task.

The king strode over to a liquor cabinet and poured himself a drink. He didn't offer us one. A calculated move—everything with him was calculated. He strode to the sitting area and took a seat, motioning us forward with his hand before propping an ankle on his knee, leaning back, the epitome of ease. Feigned ease.

I took a seat across from him, aware of Rixon's presence. My wielder didn't sit, he remained standing. It's what any wielder would have done. He certainly played the role well, when he wasn't barking commands at me in the bedroom.

The king gave a quiet snort, aware of his son's position. "How does it feel," he said to me, "making Raeria's prince subservient to you? A no-name-witch, and you've got him crawling on hands and knees."

"Oh," I huffed. "It feels incredible. Especially when he's on his knees."

A tug at our bond—a silent, smug snort—came from Rixon.

The king sneered, looking me over. Even sitting, he had mastered the ability to peer down his nose. "I always knew my son had his faults, but I never imagined he'd stoop so low."

"Yes, it illustrates the lengths he was willing to go, doesn't it? To escape his father—his crown. I can't imagine what that says about *you*. Except, I don't *need* to imagine."

Again, I offered him a cutting smile.

"Enough of this, Lady Witch. If you wish to play games, I'll match you word for word."

"I'm certain of it."

He took a sip of his drink, regarding me. Silence stretched out before us. If he was hoping to intimidate me, to make me uncomfortable, he could keep trying. At last, he said, "I submitted a formal request to the Citadel to have my city cleared of demons."

"You already have witches for that. Surely they are plenty capable."

"Oh, certainly. And yet, there are still demons roaming my city. Killing my citizens. Why, then, is that the case?" He lifted an eyebrow, letting his words sink in. "Could it be," he wondered aloud, "that the Citadel witches *aren't* doing the job they're here to do?"

"What are you implying, *Your Majesty*?"

"What do you think I'm implying, *Aramina*?"

"That there is some sort of conspiracy against you, *Maddox*, orchestrated by the Citadel's witches."

"You said it, not I."

I rolled my eyes. "Your walls are Nebrine. There shouldn't be demons in your city." And therein lay the issue. A fact I couldn't wrap my head around. Not unless...

A malicious grin split across Maddox Kozma's face, stretching his thin skin. "My thoughts, exactly." He propped his arm along the back of the sofa, rubbing his thumb against the fabric. "Tell me. Is it true that witches can draw fancy little stars and summon the creatures straight from hell?"

I hesitated, my blood running cold. Of course he would know something of our abilities. He was, after all, the king, even if the Citadel *did* operate as a separate entity outside of the king-dom's hold.

"You're suggesting that our witches are summoning demons right here in the city and using them to kill your citizens?"

He shrugged again. "I have no desire for a war with the Citadel."

The chill creeping over me turned icy. "I do not believe the Citadel desires that either, Your Majesty."

"Oh? Are you an expert on the matter? Privy to the council's wishes?"

"I..."

He had me. I wasn't—of course I wasn't. I didn't hold a posi-tion of merit, despite the possibility that I someday might. I had no idea what truly happened behind closed doors. For all my independence, I went where I was assigned, naive to the inner workings of the council.

Again, the king shrugged. "Anyway, it was just a thought. I'm sure with your...*exceptional abilities*, you'll get to the bottom of it. I did tell them to send their best. I hear you closed an entire rift."

It was my turn to shrug. "Your citizens will sleep more soundly at night, knowing they are less likely to get eaten while they travel."

"How magnanimous of you, Lady Witch."

"Indeed. You're welcome."

He ignored my jab, his gaze falling once more on his son. Again, that tick in his forehead appeared. Rixon had told me a little of his childhood. I knew that his mother had died in childbirth. Did he unfairly blame him? Resent him? Was it what he saw, every time he looked at his son?

"I see my son cannot be bothered to speak."

"He speaks when I permit him to," I snapped, some of my patience wearing thin.

"Of course. His leash. Well then, I think we're done here. Fix my city, Lady Witch. I'd hate to inform the Citadel that its witches are incompetent. Or worse, that these demons are a product of their making."

My skin heated, but I let the accusation drop. Never mind his earlier threat, that he'd make me wish I'd left. I rose, offering him a bow of my head. "I bid you a good evening, Your—"

"Oh, before I forget," he said, interrupting me as we both stood. "Since you insist on staying, while you are here you are my guests. You may come and go as you wish. My son is permitted whatever requests he deems necessary, assuming he isn't *entirely* mute. *But* you will present yourselves at dinner each night. My table, of course." My eyes narrowed. "If my son is to be your pet, I'd like to see his face while he's here." His eyes darted to Rixon once more. The vein in his forehead ticked. "Now then. Good evening, Lady Witch, Aleksander."

I didn't bother with a response. Instead, I turned and marched from the room, Rixon on my heels. I didn't speak again until we entered his chambers. Nor did I speak until I warded the door and walls, to ensure our conversations would be private. Then, only then, did I turn to my wielder and say, "What the actual *fuck*, Rixon?!"

CHAPTER 6

RIXON

Rixon paced the length of the sitting area. She'd done well, his lady witch. Unbelievably well. Her cutting responses, her defense of him, left him aching for her. But that was trumped by the king's—his *father's*—accusations.

"It can't be true," Mina said, repeating herself for the umpteenth time.

"For all we know, it could be," he said, running a hand through his hair. The tie had already fallen out, forgotten somewhere on the plush rug beneath his feet.

"He told us nothing," she snorted. "Absolutely nothing. No information about how many demons, number of deaths, nothing. To be fair, I didn't ask. I was too..." She pressed her lips together.

"Perhaps that is information we can get from the other witches."

She nodded. "We need to meet them first thing in the morning."

He hesitated, considering. "The palace walls, like the city walls, are made of Nebrine. Demons cannot cross through Nebrine walls."

"You think they're being summoned within the city?"

"That seems the only possible way. Question is, who?"

Mina sighed, slumping against the sofa. "I suppose there's only one way to find out."

He froze, turning to her. "Are you proposing we go hunting, Lady Witch?"

She scrubbed a hand over her face. "Gods, I'm so tired, Rix."

A challenging grin pulled at his lips. "If you wish, I can leave you to nap, take a look around the city, report back what I find."

She jolted upright, her body tensing like a bow string. "Absolutely not. I'm not letting you out of my sight. Not until I understand what we're up against." He lifted an eyebrow, hiding the sudden warmth seeping through his chest. "What?" she demanded. "It's not that you're incapable. It's just...Oh, stop *looking* at me like that! So what if I'm overprotective of you?"

"Mmm-hmm."

She scoffed, jumping to her feet. "Your father's playing games," she muttered under her breath, almost too quiet to hear. "I'm going to find out what they are."

She strode to the door, snatched her cloak from the peg, and threw it around her shoulders. "Well, Lord Wielder? Are you coming?"

He glanced down, adjusting the straps of his baldric, ensuring his blades were secure and accounted for. "Very well, Lady Witch. Let's go hunting."

Rixon led Mina through the city, sticking to the main roads. The eerie silence set his teeth grinding. He'd been through plenty of cities at night, but none so large as the capital with its tens of thousands. Every one of them had boasted a vibrant nightlife. That made this even stranger. It was as if Corinna held its breath. Waiting...watching.

In a city such as this, there should have been late night revelers. People strolling home from the pub. Performances at the theater. Formal dinners. Instead, the buildings and homes glowed, but no one dared set foot outside, save a few clusters of guards. They'd already dodged several pairs. It was easier than answering repetitive questions.

It might have been his birth place, but aside from a few familiar sights, much of the capital was foreign to him. There had not been much opportunity to explore as a child. That part of his life had always felt so long and drawn out. He frowned, glancing into the dark mouth of an alley.

Mina kept pace beside him. "What is it? What's the matter?"

"Nothing. I...I just realized that I've now spent more time away than I did growing up here."

Her expression softened, but she didn't say anything.

"What do you feel?" He asked after a stretch. "Anything?"

She slowed to a stop, glancing about as she pulled her long cloak tightly around her shoulders. They stood on a main thoroughfare, in a residential district now. There were side streets separating blocks, any of which might hold dangers.

She rubbed her chest. "The pressure hasn't changed, but I don't feel what I did earlier, with the Tharns. It's like, there's a promise of demons but...they aren't here." She turned in place, completing a full circle.

His lips flattened, eyes darting up and down the street.

After a deep inhale, Mina began walking again. "Come. Tell me about the city," she said. "What you know? What you remember?" The question was uncertain, as if she were afraid to voice it. His fault, because he'd turned down so many attempts in the past.

"All right." He tried to hide his hesitance.

After a moment's consideration, he took Mina's hand and led her back the way they'd come, toward one of the merchant districts, *Ivory Row*, for its whitewashed buildings. As they walked, he recalled everything he knew about Corinna. Mina listened, humming with interest.

With more than fifty thousand residents and growing, the capital city was approximately three miles from one end to the other. On foot, it took more than an hour to traverse its span. Because it was situated on the river *Runnel*, dumping straight into the sea, it received a great deal of sea trade. This allowed it to prosper despite the near disappearance of land trade.

"And what about fresh water, things like that?" Mina asked.

He hesitated. "City wells, situated throughout in the poorer areas. The richer districts had pipes laid when the city was conceived. There are tributaries, sewage, et cetera." At this, Mina frowned, then nodded. Her eyes were in constant motion, darting about, studying everything.

They walked further, dodging another pair of guards, hiding in the shadows of a nearby alley. Once they continued, Mina said, "What I find *strange* is that there are more attacks at night than during the day."

"Yes, it is odd. The demons we've encountered have never shown an aversion to daylight." She hummed. "If the witches are responsible—and I'm not saying they are—could they be summoning at night?" He hated to voice the concern, but...

A strangled laugh fell from her lips. "It would certainly explain things. I hardly know what to believe. We're playing your father's game, Rixon. He could be framing us. But that would mean he needs a witch of his own, loyal to him, to summon. It's knowledge only council witches have... supposedly." She inhaled before adding, "What if we've got it backwards?"

"What do you mean?"

"I never saw the council as aggressors. But...could it be that they are trying to start a war with the king?" She pulled her lower lip between her teeth, brows drawn. "Too much of it doesn't add up."

He grunted. Too much, indeed. It hurt his head even considering the politics of it.

His eyes swept the street and he caught a familiar sight. "Here," he said, pulling her to a stop. It was a tailor's shop. *Downing's* was written on the large sign above the door. "I used to have garments made by Marvin Downing. Not right here—he would come to the palace with his assistants. But...this is his shop."

He'd always liked the male. It was something of his childhood that hadn't been tarnished by his father. Just like his time in the stables with the stable master.

Mina's gaze swept over the shop.

There were mannequins in the window wearing all manner of designs. Even in the dim light, the gowns and doublets boasted a fine make. Nothing that would survive a witch and wielder's lifestyle in the wilderness.

Mina lifted a hand, trailing a fingertip down the glass. "They're...beautiful." Her words came out breathy. He found his eyes pinned on her face. Her throat bobbed. "When...when I was a girl, there were dances held in my town. We'd get dressed up. It was always a riot. So much fun. It wasn't until I was older, just before...everything...that I started caring about boys."

He snorted. Mostly to hide the sudden burning in his chest. It was completely unfounded, of course. The thought of her, even as a young girl, wanting to attract the attention of anyone but him, rankled.

"What?" she teased, poking his side. "It wasn't as if I *chased* any of them. They were always quick to look at my sister before me. She was the beauty."

What he *didn't* say was that he disagreed. He'd seen her sketches, crafted with expert care. Mina would always be the most beautiful thing to him.

"But..." Mina continued. "Well, I secretly harbored a desire to be noticed. I remember...it was the last dance before I lost my family—a big one. I forget why. There was a boy who'd smiled at me in town. When it came time, I *begged* Mama for a new gown. Gods, I acted so childish, until she finally relented. She had the dressmaker in town make alterations to a premade I'd seen in a fancy window just like this one, just so I'd have it in time. A beautiful, pale pink number, with dark maroon embroidery along the hem." Her face took on a far away look. An urge to see her in it crawled across his skin. "Anyway, I thought it was the most exquisite thing. I wasn't one for gowns, you know?" She turned, arching an eyebrow.

"No!" He feigned surprise. "I never would have guessed. Here I thought you were managing horses all day with frilly skirts and corsets."

"Oh, stop." She swatted his chest with the back of her hand. "Just because I enjoyed getting mussed up with the horses, didn't mean I didn't equally enjoy getting prettied up every once in a while."

He grinned. "Never said it didn't."

She fell silent, turning to look at the window again. "That gown didn't hold a candle to these. I've never seen anything quite so beautiful."

"Why don't we stop here tomorrow and have you fitted?"

A flash of longing crossed her features, lips parting, and suddenly, he wanted more than anything to buy her every damned gown in the shop. He pulled her against him, bringing their lips together. The wet warmth of her mouth, the softness of her lips, sent his mind sputtering. He flicked his tongue out and—

She stiffened.

He snorted. "Not interested in my kiss, Lady Witch?"

"Quiet," she hissed, eyes going immediately black. And he knew—*knew* exactly what she was about to say. "Follow me."

She took off at a sprint. He kept close on her heels, letting her lead. She was tracking darkness through the city. Here he'd hoped they might not be so lucky tonight.

A pair of guards materialized. "You there! Stop!"

Mina raced right past them. He didn't bother to say a word, just ran right by. Their shouts followed, as did the sound of their boots, keeping pace, block after block. At last, Mina came to a stop, her hands falling to her knees, breathing hard as she looked between two different directions.

The guards caught up. "The crime for—"

He straightened. "I am well aware of the crime for flouting curfew," he drawled. Then he removed his glove and held up his hand. It would save time.

Their eyes widened. "King said the curfew applies to all. Even witches and wielders."

Now *that* was interesting. He filed the information away for later, when he had time to analyze the implications of it.

"The king can go fuck himself," he growled. One of them gasped. The other reached for his sword.

"Oh for the gods' sake!" Mina cried, turning towards them. "He's the king's *son*, you idiots. *Your* crown prince. He's allowed to talk about his father however he wishes. Put your weapons away, there are demons loose in the city, and I intend to find them before they do irreversible damage. You louts may come along, if you wish. Otherwise, sod off."

The grumble of his laughter was impossible to stop. "As you can see, my lady witch doesn't have patience for you tonight." He disregarded them, turning to Mina. "Which way?"

She pointed. "There," and took off at a run. Feet pounded after them. Despite what Mina had said, the guards weren't interested in *sodding off*.

A frenzied barking rent the air, sending chills over his skin. "Xastors," Mina hissed. Their demonic yips echoed off buildings several blocks away. Behind him, the two guards swore, picking up their pace.

He saw the creatures before they saw him, slamming their bodies against a door, clawing at it, trying to break through. There were three of them. It was a poor district, where the homes hugged the street, with just a narrow strip of walking path before them. He heard shouts behind doors, saw faces in windows. The demons were frenzied—

Suddenly, they stopped.

One of them lifted its head, sniffed the air, then howled. The hairs on his neck prickled. As a unit, they turned their red eyes upon Mina. Demons preferred witch blood. But it was more than that. Something lived inside her. Something...*other*. They sensed it, too.

He blinked—

"Rixon!" she commanded, not bothering to draw her twin blades. He pulled his sword free.

Three Xastors would be nothing. She could have left them entirely to him, not bothered to lift a finger, and he would have managed without breaking a sweat. But instead, she subdued at the same speed as he swung. The dog-like demons fell still with Mina's magic. He removed three heads successively with the kind of precision others could only admire.

Muddled curses echoed behind him. The guards.

Mina made quick word of incinerating the leftovers. Windows swung open, heads popped out, as people regarded her, curious looks upon their faces. Several things began to add up, but he didn't mention them. Instead, he turned to the guards. "Unless you have something useful to add, you'd best be on your way." His voice left no room for argument. They were breathing hard, clearly not in the same kind of shape he and Mina were.

Demon hunting had its perks.

They nodded, still eyeing him with uncertain scrutinization. He didn't take their lack of address personally. Didn't give two shits that they weren't bowing and simpering.

"Are you all right, Lady Witch?" He kept his voice low. She nodded, studying the place the demons had ceased to exist. When at last she looked up, most of the prying faces had found somewhere else to be.

He waited until they walked out of earshot to say, "The curfew. The king isn't allowing witches to roam the streets at night. The guards at the gate scorned us. It can't be coincidental, none of it."

Her brow furrowed.

They turned down a side street, slowing their pace. "No. I don't suppose it is," she said, her voice sounding far away. "But, we will get to the bottom of it, one way or another. I have a job to do, Rixon. And I intend to do it."

He merely nodded, and they continued their hunt.

CHAPTER 7

MINA

I nestled deeper into the warmth of my wielder, pressing my hips against Rixon's thigh. Sleep pulled me under again, in fits and starts, a tug of war, until I came alert. Against me, the steady rise and fall of Rixon's chest told me he slept on.

There'd been more dreams of the winged creature. I'd only seen a mere glimpse of it, seconds amidst the chaos of the rift, months ago. And yet, when I dreamt of it, I saw it perfectly. The details of its membranous wings, the claws at the tips, its naked body, skin so gray it was nearly black. There hadn't been anything to tell it apart from male or female. In my dreams, I'd never spied any reproductive genitalia.

Which, of course, made me wonder how they reproduced.

Rixon shifted against me. The hard length of him rested against my hip. I pressed my nose against his warm chest, smiling to myself, then slid hungry fingers along his skin. He came awake with a start. Rixon wasn't a heavy sleeper, but when we were together, protected by warded doors and Nebrine walls, he let his guard slip.

I grabbed his hardened shaft, thick and rigid, and gave it a firm stroke. He groaned, pulling me tighter against him, dragging me up until our lips met. I worked him, nice and tight the way he liked. "Fuck," he mumbled against my skin.

Last night, we'd stayed out until the wee hours of the morning. Both of us too exhausted for much else beyond sleep, shedding our clothes and tumbling into bed. There'd been no further demon sightings after the Xastors. The pressure in my chest was constant, but it hadn't hitched the way it did when they were close.

I pumped Rixon again. At the top of my stroke, I swirled my thumb over the head of his cock, already beading with pearly liquid. I spread it around and he groaned again. "Put your hands on the headboard, Lord Wielder. You are not to touch me this time."

"Mina—" His voice was sleep roughened.

"*Hand's above your head,*" I commanded. He released me at once. His palms went flush to the headboard. I let my eyes linger on his arms, the way his muscles strained and bulged with restraint, forearms covered in thickened veins. He tested the bond, pulled against it.

A deep, rough chuckle rumbled from his chest. "My little witch wants to play? All right, put those pretty lips around my cock and play. Suck me good. I want to come in your mouth."

My stomach swooped. I blinked, then tried to reorder my thoughts. "You aren't in a position to make *demands*," I managed, recovering from the delicious desire licking through me.

"Let me see your eyes," he hissed, when I gave his cock a stroke that was near painful. "I want them black—black for me, Mina."

The order swept through me. He might hold the bond, he might not possess its power as I did, but *gods*, he had a way of controlling me. There was something about the authority in his voice that made me desperate to fall on my knees, to behave like a good girl, and grant his every wish.

I felt the demonic thing twisting inside me. It surged to the surface, rising to the occasion. Sensual claws scraped down my spine, made me shiver. I moved, settling between Rixon's corded legs, lowering onto my thighs, bringing my mouth to him.

His chest rose and fell. I sucked him harder and he swore. With each stroke of my mouth, of my tongue, his low growls dictated my movement. It didn't take long—it never did— before his cock hardened beyond belief. I felt his body tighten while I played with him. He was close—so close. His hips gave a final thrust. A garbled sentence fell from his mouth. Something about how fucking beautiful I was, or some sort.

Salty male essence spurted into my mouth.

I swallowed him down, every last drop, using my tongue to lick him clean. I didn't release him until I was completely satisfied with my thoroughness. Then I discarded my leash.

Hands free, he flipped our positions, his movements fast and practiced. "How does it feel when the tables are turned?" he purred, parting my thighs, settling between them. "Hmm, little witch? How does it feel to be at *my* mercy?"

I groaned, falling prey to the press of his body, to the feel of his erection probing my wet folds. "What makes you certain the tables have turned, Lord Wielder?" My voice pitched low, not quite my own. A mixture of new and old, reflecting the *thing* that lived inside me. A darkness I still couldn't explain.

"Oh, they've turned," he affirmed. He grabbed my wrists, holding them above my head. I struggled against him, albeit half-hearted. He would always outmatch me in strength; I was completely helpless against this male. Herrin's immaculate training, my abilities to wield a blade and use my fists to defend myself, slipped away.

My core clenched, needy. "I am entirely at your mercy," I rasped. "What will you do to me?"

"Wicked, *wicked* things." Already he was at my entrance, the head of him pressing but not entering. Then his mouth found mine and claimed it, tongue lashing against my own. I was slick and desperate. With his free hand, he ran the head of his cock over my folds, up and back, up and back. My thighs began to tremble. Each time he hit the bundle of nerves at my apex, I tightened, groaning, willing my body to orgasm.

"You see how my cock makes you, little witch?" he asked. "You see how desperate? How needy?"

"Mmm!"

"That's how you make me feel, just looking at you."

A gasp fell from my lips. He released himself and twisted his free hand into my hair, claiming my mouth again. I was so tight, so eager for release; my body quivered with suppressed need.

He took me with a single thrust. The power of his hips left me gasping. I groaned, drowning beneath the sensation of him, clenching tight.

"Oh no, little hellion. Relax that cunt. I don't want you coming anytime soon." I gave a mew of protest, nearly sobbing with frustration, garbled words. "I said, *relax it*," he commanded. The hand around my wrists tightened, sending a spear of pain along my arms.

I cried out—shocked.

Rixon froze. His face changed in an instant, softening, like he was about to release me—

"No," I hissed. "Don't stop. Do it again."

I *liked* it. I didn't want him afraid. I didn't want him cautious.

He hesitated a second more, then nodded. The hand around my wrists tightened again, past the point of pain, enough to make my eyes water. I squirmed beneath him, not to break free, never to break free. He'd turned me into a needy, desperate creature, after all.

His hips retreated, then slammed down again. I cried out, clenching. Each time I did, he froze, halting the potential orgasm I begged for. "If you tighten up, you come. I told you *no*," he snarled, voice matching the thing inside me. Each scolding was accompanied by a painful squeeze of his hand on my wrists. If I hadn't been a witch, there would be awful purple bruises left behind.

As it was, it only took twice more for me to learn how to behave. Each time I clenched around him, he withheld and hurt me. He was *training* me. And I? I had suddenly become the world's most compliant student.

Breathing hard, I forced my walls to relax, forcing myself to keep from tightening each time he swept in. A different kind of euphoric pleasure began to take hold, tingles starting at the base of my spine. Soon, tears slid down my temples. I tried. I tried *so hard* not to tighten up.

"That's it, little demon. That's a good girl. Just like that," he praised, making me glow with pride. And then he gave a thrust that ended me, sweeping in, grinding hard against my clit. It took me by surprise. My body spasmed before my mind caught up, wave after wave of pleasure breaking over me.

"Fuck," he growled, realizing what he'd done. And then, he was pumping into me. Emptying himself for my taking. And take, I did. Every last drop.

It was...incomprehensible.

When he settled down, pulling me into his arms, I continued to tremble. His hands were gentle as he swept them over my skin, caressing. He brushed loose strands of hair from my temple, kissing my damp forehead, humming with delight.

We lay there in the quiet morning confines of his suite, the sounds of our mingled breath twisting together. I trailed my fingers over his scars, at last capturing one of his hands as he tried to tickle me, twining our fingers together. I played with his palm, running my thumb over the skin. He had a deep scar that ran diagonally over the flesh. I traced it, as I often did when we held hands, then pulled my fingers away. "What demon gave you this one?"

"Hmm?" His voice was lazy, laced with the aftermath of his orgasm.

"Your scar here?" He had scars everywhere, wounds he'd picked up under the care of his former. Ena had mistreated him abominably, and almost never healed him as punishment. It was one of the reasons he'd been so wary during our initial days.

"Oh." He shrugged against me. "That's left over from my childhood, actually."

I hesitated, treading very, very carefully. "I thought I knew all your scars. How...how did you manage this one?"

"Probably doing some stupid shit or another. Don't remember, actually."

"You must have been very young. It...it wasn't your father, was it?" My stomach twisted.

"No. Certainly not. He was only physically abusive with his fists. Never a blade, or anything like that."

I could have wept with relief, that he would admit this in light of his recent moods. But he had, and I refused to make a big deal of it. Instead, I made a humming noise and said, "It looks deep." I lifted it closer to my face. Had it been fresh, I could have healed it; there wouldn't have been a scar.

Unlike most witches, I had received specialized healer's training from Juna, the witch in charge of the Citadel's infirmary. As witches and wielders in training, we'd all been exposed to demons in controlled environments. But it was our wielders that took the brunt of the injuries. Before going out into the world, they faced them in special sparring rings outfitted with summoning stars, closed in with the beasts to learn how to fight them. Most of the time, they suffered wounds.

While all witches learned how to heal common maladies, flesh wounds and the like, I learned so much more. I could set bones, knit vital organs back together, and even reattach parts like fingers and toes. It had required more than just practice, but a thorough understanding of the human body. Hours spent pouring over texts to better understand how the lungs worked, how the intestines functioned—

A loud knock startled us both from our silent thoughts. "Breakfast, Your Highness," a voice called.

I groaned and rolled over. "If I weren't so hungry, I'd tell him to fuck off."

Rixon merely hummed. I rose and snagged a robe, padding through the suite to remove the wards from the door and admit the servants. Rixon didn't bother rising, but he did cover himself with a sheet. When I glanced back, he had an arm propped under his head, the other resting on his chest, watching me. His expression was lazy, content.

I pulled my lower lip between my teeth, already desperate to crawl back under the covers with him. But...we needed to visit the witches, get to the bottom of things. The sooner we solved the issue, the sooner we could leave this awful place.

Well, admittedly, I actually liked the city, what I'd seen of it. I also wasn't *too* against the palace, either. It was vibrant here, beautiful, indulgent in a way I'd never been allowed to be. Too bad Rixon's father had ruined all that, soured what could have been fondness for his childhood home.

"Forgive me, Lady Witch. Your breakfast," the servant was saying. I recognized him from last night. Ansel. And sure enough, Florian scurried in right after him with a pitcher of juice.

"Just there, on the table is fine."

They sent glances in Rixon's direction. I didn't miss the grin that pulled at my wielder's lips as they saw him there, broad chest on display, sheet pooled at his waist. He was enjoying this.

As soon as the servants set out the food, they scurried away, shutting the door behind them. I strode to the table and looked over the faire. "Boiled eggs, oatmeal, bacon, fruit, and toast with jam and honey," I called out, pleased. Then I took a seat and began fussing with it.

"Too eager to wait for me?" Rixon appeared behind me, leaning over my chair, burying his nose against my neck. "I could feed you, if you like?"

He loved feeding me, and the casual way he asked didn't cover up what I already knew. "Well, all right then. Sit down."

He'd stolen the sheet from the bed, wrapped it around his waist, tucked it in. I couldn't help my eyes, lingering on the hair that shot straight down to his cock, now hidden, and the rigid muscles flexing as he lowered himself into the chair.

I bolted up and rounded the table, plopping into his lap. He chuckled, scooting the tray towards us. I began pouring juice as he arranged the spread.

He started with the bacon, feeding me straight from his fingers. Every brush of my lips against his thumb had heat blossoming low in my gut. We'd only just fucked and I was already on edge again. The thing inside me was insatiable.

It was erotic, the way he saw to my needs. We devoured everything on the tray. Rixon always had an ample appetite. Never one to turn down food. Where he put it, I couldn't say. "It doesn't even turn to fat," I groused. "It just makes your muscles bigger and bigger."

Not so for me. It just pooled in my thighs. I *did* have generous thighs and hips, even if I didn't have large breasts. But, Rixon had made it abundantly clear that he loved everything about me, exactly as it was.

"All the better to protect you with, my love," he cooed, rubbing his nose against the side of my jaw before taking the juice goblet and chugging it down. "Now, we have business to address. You want a bath, I take it?"

I snorted. "I'm covered in cum. So, yes."

"But I like you covered in me," he purred.

"It's sticky," I tsked.

"Very well." His eyes sparkled. "Let's make it fast."

And by that he meant, bend me over the lip of the bathing pool so he could fuck me from behind. We *did* make it fast. There was no playing involved. He finished me in minutes before washing my hair and body. I did the same for him, and then we were dressed and striding through the palace, off to chase our quarry.

CHAPTER 8

RIXON

Rixon made a few inquiries before leaving the palace. The Citadel witches were staying at an inn called the *King's Mantle*. Mina had snorted, at that. Apparently his father hadn't been gracious enough to host them in the palace. He wasn't surprised in the slightest. His father had never liked witches. Perhaps that was partly why he'd found himself in the Citadel, all those years ago; it had given him secret satisfaction.

Considering his father's biting words last night, about how he'd stooped so low, the blade had hit the mark. But his father had it all wrong. There'd been no stooping, well, except when he was on his knees for her. No, to claim her, it had been all striving and plotting and reaching. He was damned lucky she'd chosen him. He hadn't known *how* lucky, that first day when they'd bonded. But now? Now, he knew. And fuck if he didn't want to drop to his knees, here and now, and thank her for it.

It was a short walk, in a nicer part of the city, a few blocks from *Ivory Row*. Marvin Downing's shop wasn't far, either. A sudden thought came to mind. He saved it for later.

The streets were busy this time of day, people rushing about, trying to complete errands. With curfew at nightfall, there was less time in the day to get things done. Most passersby didn't pay him any mind, except the few gaping at his weapons. He was dressed like a well armed commoner, not a prince.

"It's rather quaint, isn't it?" Mina asked, stopping before the *King's Mantle*. It was a square, white-washed building with navy blue window shutters and picturesque planter boxes beneath each one. It stood five levels tall. There was a large garden in front, gated, for its patrons. A small porch was occupied by several of them, in rocking chairs.

He opened the garden gate and they strode down the path and into the inn. The entryway was inviting and grand, with high ceilings and a crystal chandelier. His boots sank into a plush rug, intricately woven in reds and golds. They found an attendant behind a desk. A mousy woman with gray hair and spectacles.

Through an archway on his left, there was a dining room with clusters of tables and several late diners, eating breakfast. An arch on his right led to a comfortable common room with a fireplace at one end. Already, there were clusters of people, some with books in hand, others chatting.

"How may I help you, sir? Madam?" The attendant looked between them.

"Oh, hello," Mina said, stepping forward, inquiring after the witches residing within the inn.

The attendant caught sight of Mina's hand, her markings, and directed them into the common room. "Through there," she said. "And please let me know if I can be of any further assistance, Lady Witch."

Mina strode through the arched doorway, glancing around. He stayed close on her heels. At first, nothing happened, then several conversations fell silent. "Don't tell me the king placed an order for *more* of us," a voice drawled.

Mina covered the distance, approaching the cluster of witches. "He certainly did," she answered, coming to a stop beside an occupied cluster of furniture. "Hello."

There were four witches and two wielders. They sat in a circle on sofas and chairs closest to the large fireplace. Everyone's eyes fell on him, not Mina. For a moment, it caught him off guard. Wielder's were generally beneath notice among witches.

It only took a moment to discover the reason. One of the witches said, "*So!* It's true then. We heard the rumors this morning. Not only did the king's son return, but he returned as a welder." The woman was older, late forties, perhaps? Or, early fifties? Her chestnut hair was already streaked with thin strands of silver. "Brilliant. Just, brilliant. And you, dear?"

"Aramina. Mina for short. And this is my wielder, Rixon."

"I thought the prince's name was Aleksander?" one of the other witches pipped up. She was younger, perhaps late twenties, with caramel skin and curly black hair that framed her face with tight coils.

Mina smiled at her. "Aleksander Rixon Kozma. He prefers Rixon, but you may address him as Lord Wielder or Your Highness."

The youngest girl, a curvy blonde with a round, friendly face, burst into fits of laughter. "Oh, I bet the king is *falling over* with fury. His own son! A loathsome wielder. What can he be thinking about *that*?!"

Mina's mouth twitched in response to the obvious sarcasm. She said, "I assure you, he's quite beside himself with disgust." In a matter of seconds, these witches had put her at ease. It wasn't anything like when they'd encountered Helena, Ena's best friend.

"Well, come, sit, let us have introductions. I'm afraid some of our group are currently away, but I'm sure you'll meet them later. Are you staying here at the inn, dear? Did Margaret get you set up with rooms?"

"Oh." Mina hesitated. "Actually, we're staying at the palace."

"The palace? Right under the king's nose!" said the woman with the curly black hair. Her eyes danced with mirth. "How very delightful."

"That's Elianna," said the witch who appeared to be the matriarch.

"Pleasure to meet you, Elianna," Mina said.

"Viktor is out—my wielder—otherwise I'd introduce you." Elianna shrugged, like it was no matter. She shifted over, patting the space beside her. "But you can sit with me. I don't bite."

Mina accepted. He waited to see her settled before striding across the room and snatching a wooden chair. He carried it over and flipped it around, straddling it. From his place at the edge of the circle, he had a good vantage point of the entire room.

"Well then. My name is Mya," said the oldest witch. "I've been keeping this lot in line for years. They come and go, occasionally, taking other assignments. But Josette—she's out at the moment—has been here nearly as long as I have."

"I'm Anne," the curvy blonde spoke up. "Got assigned here a few years ago."

"I...I think I remember seeing you in the Citadel," Mina said.

"You probably did," said Anne, smiling, pleased to be remembered. "I only bonded with my wielder three years ago."

"And the quiet one there," Mya said, "is Lola. That's her wielder, Julian."

"Pleasure to meet you, Lola, Julian," said Mina. They both offered her nods.

"The *other* brute there is *my* wielder," Mya continued. "Flynn." Mina nodded in greeting towards Flynn, who gave a bob of his head.

Rixon hadn't met either wielder. They hadn't crossed paths in his time at the Citadel, nor in the wild, and since Flynn had been stationed here for what appeared decades, it wasn't a surprise.

He couldn't help the way his eyes lingered over the wielders present. It was a natural inclination, to size himself up. After years of training in a competitive atmosphere, the habit was hard to break.

"Josette and Odell will be back later, as are Ronan—that's Anne's wielder—Cayden, Lucas, and Viktor."

"I look forward to meeting them," Mina said, politely. "Now, what can you tell me about the demons in the city?"

"Oh!" A laugh burst from Anne's lips. Her cup of tea stalled before it reached her mouth. "I like her already. Straight and to the point."

"Be quiet, Anne," Elianna admonished. "Not everyone prefers your level of frivolous conversation, darling."

Anne merely shrugged a shoulder.

"Well," said Mya, turning serious. "It's a horrible thing, what's happening here. Demons roaming city streets. Witches forced to leave them be, or suffer the consequences. Humans pay the price. It all started about eight weeks ago? Give or take?"

"No issues before that?"

"Never," said Mya. "Been here a long time. Never saw a demon within the city before that. It started slow. A couple demons cropping up, here and there."

"Huh." Mina scowled. "And now?"

"A daily occurrence."

"Daily?!" Anne snorted. "Nightly, Mother Mya!" Anne glanced at Mina, adding, "She's not really my mother, she just mother-hens us."

Mya sighed, long and drawn out. "Anne is correct. They usually appear around or after nightfall. King imposed the curfew almost as soon as it started."

Rixon caught Mina's gaze. A knowing look passed between them. It was too coincidental.

"We disregarded the curfew at first," Mya added, "going out at night to hunt them."

"At first?"

"Well...breaking curfew is grounds for arrest. Guards threw us in the cells." At this, Mina's lips parted in surprise. Mya continued, "They weren't gentle with us, either. Didn't care that this is our *duty*—slaying demons, keeping people safe. Didn't care that witches operate outside the king's laws.

"We fought back, in a way. Snuck out when we could. Eventually, we just got tired of it." Mya sighed. "Sometimes, I feel the king deserves to see his city crumble. But...well, then I remind myself that it's the citizens who suffer. Isn't exactly their fault, now is it?"

"So...you've just...given up?" Mina's brows pulled tight.

"Oh, we're still helping where we can, within the limitations of the king's rules. We go out at first light, kill whatever survives 'till morning."

"Why haven't you simply fought back?" Mina asked. "Witches, wielders, we are more powerful than the guards."

"Can you imagine how that will look, dear? Us maiming the king's guards because we broke the rules? No, this is a political game the king is playing, Lady Witch."

Mya had a valid point.

"My father likes to play games." The words were out before Rixon realized he'd spoken. Heads turned towards him in surprise. Wielders, as a rule, let the witches do the talking. He'd gotten used to Mina's company, used to her treating him as an equal.

"The king hates us," Lola said after an awkward beat of silence, speaking for the first time. She was a skinny thing, middle aged, with big eyes and dirty blond hair.

"So do the people. They think it's *our* fault they're dying," said Anne, rolling her eyes. "It's the king they ought to blame."

Rixon frowned as a picture crystalized in his mind. The king imposed a curfew, forcing witches to adhere to it. As a result, demons ran wild. People suffered, creating animosity between them. No wonder Mina had received such scorn yesterday.

It still didn't answer the biggest question of all. Who was summoning the demons? Moreover, why were they more frequently appearing at night? Certainly, it was easy to pin this on his father, until he considered such a crucial aspect.

Only witches carried the knowledge of summoning stars, and there were six known witches living here within the city, right here under this very roof. It would be shortsighted to assume they had nothing to do with this. Not without solid proof. Mina felt the same way, given that she hadn't voiced all of her concerns.

"Curfew or not," Mina said at last, "I don't intend to sit back and allow the king his games. We went hunting last night. Brought down three Xastors." She detailed exactly what had happened, making it clear that they would continue prowling the streets at night; the king wouldn't dare arrest his own heir.

The rest of their time passed quickly. Mina relayed all she could about recent events at the Citadel, what they'd encountered on their journey across Raeria, and what they'd found in Rockfall. She kept certain details out, naturally, namely her own changes.

At one point, tea and cakes were served, and at another, the remaining witches and wielders returned, prompting more introductions. At last, they began saying their goodbyes. "I think I'll take some fresh air," Elianna announced, standing. "May I accompany you back to the palace, Mina?"

"Oh." Mina hesitated, then a soft smile spread across her lips. "I would like that—"

"Actually," Rixon interjected, "I was planning to take Mina to Downing's for a dress fitting and a few additions to her wardrobe."

Elianna gave him a curious look, her gaze darting between Rixon and Mina, surprised that Mina hadn't reacted to his interruption. A moment later, Elianna shrugged it off, saying, "Oh! I do love a good shopping spree."

"Shopping spree?!" Anne cried, flouncing over. Upright, she only came to Mina's shoulder, but what she lacked in height she made up for in generous, *very generous* curves. Rixon's lips twitched. She was rather entertaining, he decided. Both women would be good company for Mina. It probably wasn't healthy for her to rely solely on him for companionship.

"The both of you should join us," he decided. Never in a million years would he expect *those* words to fall from his lips.

"That would be splendid," Anne said. "Come, ladies. Let's go have some fun."

Mina shot him a glance, her brows lifting, as if to say, *what mischief are you up to?* He merely winked, giving a slight, reassuring tug on their bond.

They stepped out onto the city street, both women linking arms, with Mina in the middle. He followed at a distance. Ronan and Viktor fell into step beside him, immediately striking up a conversation.

He hated being social. He'd have rather slayed demons. But, he forced himself to appear amiable throughout their near interrogation into his past. Eventually, their conversation moved to weaponry and fighting styles. For this, he remained mostly silent. He often wondered if the relationships between witches and wielders was so stifling, that when wielders gathered together, they spewed all the words they'd saved up, bursting to get free.

He nearly groaned with relief when Downing's shop came into view.

"Mina," he said, interrupting Ronan's rant about the lack of skilled Nebrine smiths in the capital. "Have several gowns fitted. We've got dinner with my father tonight. You'll need one of the premade options, but beyond that, whatever you wish. Charge it to my account."

He ignored the shocked expressions on the wielders beside him, and the growing curiosity of their witches. He didn't care. He wasn't going to adjust how he acted in Mina's presence for fear of judgment or scorn.

"Your...your account?" Mina asked. He'd never told her that he had an entire inheritance in the treasury. He'd left it all behind when he ran away. But, well, there wasn't any reason to ignore it while he was here. The wages they made slaying demons wouldn't cover a single gown of Marvin Downing's. But with his treasury, she could have hundreds...if she wanted.

"My account," he confirmed. "Marvin will know."

She opened and closed her mouth, then nodded, sweeping into the shop, leaving him at the mercy of the two males in his company.

CHAPTER 9

MINA

I hadn't hidden my surprise. Rixon had seen it. But, honestly, an account? An entire account? Here we were, going on assignments, slaughtering demons, living off the pay we received, and he had an *account*?! But of course he did. He was a prince. And if the king was the richest man in the kingdom—which he probably was—then what did that make Rixon?

"Are you all right, Mina?" Anne leaned on my arm. Elianna had already moved off to examine several gowns in the shop.

"I think I feel a little dizzy," I admitted, letting out a nervous laugh.

"Here, come and sit." Anne fussed over me. I rather liked her, and Elianna too. They were complete opposites, but both had an excellent sense of humor. Anne was ultra talkative—which is why Rixon's invitation to bring them had surprised me—whereas Elianna was more reserved and level headed.

Having a bench under my rump grounded me. Anne patted my arm. "They're now. Was it all the city noise? That often gets to *my* head. For someone who has been in the wilderness, it's a bit much."

"No. No, it wasn't that." I wasn't ready to admit why.

"This will look splendid on you, Mina," Elianna said, spinning over holding a gown. It was a dark blue creation with light blue accents and a golden silk sash.

"*Ah*, the mistress is correct," said a voice. We all jumped, turning towards the source. An old, squat man appeared, glasses squished against his nose. Despite a bustling shop, he'd singled us out. "Lady Witches, a pleasure. Looking for gowns today?"

"*She's* looking for a gown," Anne piped up. "Several, in fact. Her wielder out there—*Prince Aleksander Rixon Kozma*—told her to charge everything to his account."

Well, it was certainly a *not-so-subtle* name drop.

"Prince—gods above!" Marvin Downing, as I assumed him to be, stumbled back a step, looking out the window. He caught sight of Rixon's towering form beside the other two wielders.

I stood and produced my hand. "It's a pleasure to meet you, sir. My name is Mina, and yes, that is my wielder out there, Rixon."

Marvin Downing chuckled. "*Rixon*, eh? The name his mother gave him. Splendid. Just *splendid*. I used to make all his clothes when he was a young lad." He hesitated to see my reaction, then continued, more to himself. "I'll have to speak with him, yes. He's in dire need of my assistance." His eyes raked over Rixon's attire, catching on some of the weapons littering his person.

"I'm certain he'd be glad to have his measurements taken," I mentioned.

"Indeed...indeed." Marvin lapsed into thought before clapping his hands. "First things first! *You*, Lady Witch. Mina. What would you like then? The blue one there? Yes, perfect. And we shall have you measured, of course. I'd be honored to commission several pieces. It might take me a few days, but I'll have them done right. Until then, we can pick from what's here and I'll have them altered. Danny! Shay!" Two of his assistants all but sprouted into existence by his side. Like they'd done this before. "Come. We've got work to do."

I was ushered to a pedestal while Marvin barked orders, summoning bolts of fabric from his assistants. He pinned and prodded, measured and noted, pausing here and there to ask questions. Did I prefer pink to nude? Blue to purple? Silk barcode or tulle? What about pockets? How would I like the skirts adjusted for maximum mobility?

Between his questions, Elianna and Anne asked me questions about Rixon, about my life before the Citadel, about different witches. Did I know a witch named Marilyn? What about Natalie? They also tried on dresses of their own, just for fun.

I couldn't help my smile. Couldn't help as my worries were forgotten. They made me think of Tasha, my only friend in the Citadel. A sudden desire to see her, speak with her, see how her life was going, swept over me.

She'd once accused me of being too closed off, never allowing anyone to get close. She'd been right. It was *those* memories, *those* accusations that I considered when I'd finally let Rixon know me.

"We should have come to this shop ages ago," Anne sighed, wistfully. "These gowns are gorgeous."

They'd both arrived here wearing the efficient, homespun dresses that witches often wore. We were, after all, slaying demons and traipsing about the wilderness in between assignments, and more importantly, living on a meager wage. I preferred pants and a tunic, often accenting everything with a corset to show off my hips. But most witches preferred skirts they could move freely in.

"It's not as if we ever have an occasion to dress up," Elianna sighed, twirling in a deep crimson and yellow piece that set off her skin tone and warm eyes.

"The king doesn't invite you to his dinner parties?"

"Gods, no. Dinners?" Elianna snorted. "I'd die before getting stuck at one of those. All pompous nobility and fuddy-duddies," she added, dropping her voice to a whisper, since most of the people browsing were exactly that.

Marvin chuckled.

"Well," I said, "you'll have to wish me luck, then."

"You should come to the inn and dine with us," Anne said. "Far more enjoyable. We're the greatest of friends. And Mother Mya always sees that we're cared for proper."

Her invitation enticed me more than I expected. "I probably will. Not sure how I'll stand the king's company for long."

"Yes, see that you do," Anne agreed, giving a pleased nod.

I looked them over, capturing my lower lip between my teeth. It had only been a single morning, and already I was fond of them. *These* were the witches King Kozma suspected of summoning demons? Really? Neither seemed the type. I could hardly believe it.

And yet, I needed to be certain.

I considered my suspects, less inclined to think suspiciously of Anne and Elianna. Lola had been extremely quiet. Could that be evidence enough? Both Josette and Odell had been out most of the morning, doing who could say what. And what of Mya? She seemed the least likely, but could that make her an ideal candidate?

My stomach twisted. A witch betraying the citadel? It went against everything! We were trained to protect, not harm. I hated the thought.

I sighed, glancing at myself in the mirror.

I needed answers and that meant digging into the matter myself. Rixon and I had work to do. I just hoped I could handle whatever truths I discovered.

I linked my arm through Rixon's as we took up a leisurely pace through the city, keeping to the main thoroughfare. It was early afternoon, and the weather was mild, overcast. Rixon had explained that many days were like this, given the proximity to the sea. The sound of gulls overhead punctuated the city's hum. I'd always thought sea birds only dined on fish, but everywhere I looked, they swooped between buildings, cawing and collecting discarded food, digging through refuse, pattering about in gutters.

"They're dirty birds," Rixon had explained at the start of our walk. "Near as bad as pigeons."

Earlier, we'd decided to dine at a small pub near Marvin's. Everything was charged to Rixon's account, naturally. We'd had an excellent clam chowder and seared sea bass with rice and vegetables. The rice, he'd explained, was imported from across the sea. I'd only had rice a few times because of the difficulty in getting it inland. I'd eaten enough to burst. Hence, our walk.

We'd long since bid goodbye to our companions. I'd already given him an abridged version of our time in the shop, Marvin's excitement over his return, and the invitation to dine at the inn when we wished to avoid his father.

"How did you find their wielders?" I now asked, tugging on his arm. We crossed the thoroughfare and headed in the direction of the ports. Rixon grunted, shrugging. His eyes darted about, taking in every single detail. "That bad, huh?"

"They talk too much."

My laugh was more of a bark. "*Dearest* Rixon," I cooed. "Everyone talks too much, by your standards."

"Not everyone."

"Oh?"

"I never mind your conversation, Lady Witch." His eyes darted to mine, and his expression softened a measure, before he turned his gaze back to the street.

"Of course you don't, especially when it's dirty things."

"Especially not then."

"You are insufferable! You—"

"Aleksander?! Oh my gods!" I whirled around and caught a flash of red. I blinked, staggering back several steps. A female clung to my wielder, her arms wrapped around his neck.

For a moment, I simply stood there, nearly sputtering. Then, a laugh burst from my chest. The look on Rixon's face—he was positively appalled. Well, he certainly didn't find anything funny about it, not like I did. I calmed myself, plastering my hands against my mouth to hold back my laughter, as Rixon began detaching the red-headed beauty from him.

"Oh, do forgive me," she declared, finally stepping back. "It's just...I heard rumors of your return. I *so* hoped they were true. I knew you would return eventually. Father knew it too! We've been waiting so, *so* anxiously. You—"

"Forgive me, madam, but...have we met?"Rixon somehow grew taller.

The female's expression fell.

He glanced my way, looking for help, but I only took another step back. I might have interceded on his behalf, but this...this was just too much. Rixon's frown deepened.

"You...you don't remember me?" Her eyes began to glitter. "Trudy Holland? My father's Lord Diego Holland—your father's advisor."

"Oh, of course! Miss Holland," Rixon said, snapping his fingers. He didn't remember—I could see it in his expression. But hers? Hers lit up.

I suppressed a groan.

"There! I knew I'd jog your memory. We used to play together as toddlers in the nursery, until, well, until my mother died, remember? My father took me and my siblings back to Darbyfort."

"Yes. Yes of course." Rixon said. He still didn't remember. I was shaking now, trying so very hard not to let my laughter burst free. I didn't want to draw her attention. Trudy seemed oblivious of my presence. The poor thing. She only had eyes for Rixon.

She was slender, on the taller side, dressed extravagantly—her father was a lord, after all—with curly red hair the color of fire. Her hair was rather beautiful. Her age was hard to judge, but she appeared several years older than me, which would make sense, if she had played with Rixon as a toddler. He was thirty now, having recently celebrated a birthday right before we departed from Rockfall.

I glanced down at her gloved hand. She wasn't married, if she was still going by her father's surname. Odd, for a female her age, not that I was judging.

"Forgive me, Miss Holland, but I really must be going."

Trudy's face drooped. "Right. But of course. I...I hadn't meant to disturb your walk." Her eyes finally turned towards me. I offered a slow, mischievous grin. Her throat bobbed; she took a step back. Even without showing my darkness, she second-guessed any sort of introduction between us. I wasn't keen to give one, despite the comical nature of this entire situation.

"Right," she said again, smoothing her gown, looking back at Rixon. "Well, Aleksander, it was a pleasure to see you again. I am so glad for your return." With that, she bowed and turned, striding away.

Only then did I let my raucous laughter burst free. My voice echoed and I caught a glimpse of Trudy, turning to glare at me over her shoulder, before continuing on her way. That only made me laugh harder. Rixon thumped me on the back.

"Are you quite all right, Lady Witch?" he asked, sounding more annoyed than anything.

"Oh...yes...quite," I managed between gasping breaths. "The look...your face...oh, gods!"

"Yes. Thank you, for your timely assistance."

"Gods," I breathed again, finally standing upright, wiping the tears from my eyes. "You had no idea *who* that poor girl was, did you?"

"No fucking idea," he grumbled, scrubbing a hand over his face.

"Well, she certainly remembered *you*." I linked my arm through his. He merely narrowed his eyes, doing his best to glower, before we continued on towards the docks.

Poor Rixon.

I was eager to see the port. I'd seen glimpses from a few vantage points in the palace, massive apparatuses rising well above the buildings, to offload cargo from ships. But nothing prepared me for the sight when we arrived.

It reminded me of the Citadel, for how small it made me feel. Like an ant. Massive warehouses gave way to large, open areas with mountains of crates. "They're called cranes," Rixon explained when he saw me gazing, open mouthed, at the tall structures fitted with ropes and pulleys. Some of them were in use, lowering over the decks of ships, lifting clusters of goods contained within nets, swinging sideways, depositing them onto the ground.

It was a beehive of activity. People rushed about, unloading, moving, transporting. Orders were shouted, punctuating the din of conversation between employees and sailors.

It was a sight. I simply stood there, my arm in Rixon's, watching. We must have looked on for ten minutes or more, before we began to walk again.

"I'd like to see the sea, the beach, while we're here," I told him. We'd seen it in the distance, just beyond the city, when we'd rode in. It would be good for Jarrow and Farrah.

I'd never seen an ocean before, but I'd read of them plenty. Sand and salty water. I was eager.

"I think we can arrange that," Rixon mused, running his fingers over mine. I squeezed his arm in answer. Then we began making our way back to the palace.

My gown arrived just before dinner—delivered by one of Marvin Downing's assistants, flanked by two servants whom I didn't recognize. Rixon was at the new liquor cabinet, pouring himself a glass, while I removed the wrappings and held the dress against me. The back was a series of intricate buttons, at least twenty of them, for which I'd need Rixon's assistance.

I sighed at my reflection in the mirror, swishing the silk about as I held it to me. With my black hair—growing blacker by the day—the blue looked lovely. The gold sash added just the right *pop* of brightness.

I glanced over to find Rixon leaning against the sofa, watching me. His expression was unreadable, but the spark in his gaze said enough. "I believe women have handmaidens for this sort of thing," I said. "But alas, I shall have to appoint you for the job."

He snorted.

I removed my robe, letting it fall to the ground. Rixon's eyes darkened. Then I undid the buttons and slipped into the gown, pulling it up over my shoulders. It slid over my skin like a memory, reminding me of a different time, a different world. I shivered at the soft feel of it.

Growing up, the country dances I had attended were a high-light, especially as I'd approached my teenage years. Now, I had a male to enjoy me, dressed like this. Pulling my hair to the side, I turned my back to him, facing the mirror. He set his glass down and strode over.

The space between us heated.

His fingers brushed against my bare back, sending a shiver down my spine. He didn't fuss with the buttons. Instead, he laid his lips on the base of my neck, right where it met my spine. My abdominal muscles tightened. "My, my, Lady Witch." The warmth of his tongue followed his lips. He licked up the column of my neck to my hairline, the action possessive. I groaned, watching him do it in the reflection. "I'm afraid I won't get all these buttons done before I'm ready to pull this thing off you."

I captured my bottom lip between my teeth. "You could always fuck me with it on." He looked up then, eyes catching mine in the reflection. His pupils darkened. He liked the sound of that.

His fingers made quick work of the buttons, then. He was doing the last as the dinner bell began to ring. I groaned— denied. All this fussing had wetness pooling between my thighs.

Rixon pulled me against him. He ground his hips against me, letting me feel the length of his erection. "This will be waiting for later," he said against my ear, his voice a low warning. "I'm going to fuck you in this dress, Mina, with your skirts hiked around your waist."

A desperate gasp fell from my lips. I squeezed my thighs together. He glanced down at my reflection, then grabbed fistfuls of my skirt, began hiking it up, revealing my bare legs. I watched my reflection as he slipped a finger into my folds.

My breaths turned shallow.

Seeing his hand work me was almost too much. My knees weakened. He didn't let me fall, held fast to my waist, keeping me pressed against him.

Heat built, sending tingles up through the base of my spine. "Oh, gods!" I cried, voice warping, head falling against his shoulder, eyes fixed on our bodies. It was so, *so* erotic.

"You're dripping, little witch. So desperate for what only I can give you."

"Yes," I managed. "Yes!"

My eyes turned completely black, the sight sending shivers over my arms. The thing that looked back at me—it wasn't me. A slow, feral grin spread across my lips in greeting.

Rixon began working me harder, until my hips met his thrusts. "That's it, little demon. Claim your pleasure. I love when you fuck my hand." The demonic power in me surged. My body tightened around him, clenching, as my pleasure built and then—

He ripped his hand away. "No...no no no," I screeched, trying to grab it, to capture it in mine, trying to put it back where it belonged. The promise of my orgasm fragmented and disappeared.

He brought his slick fingers to his lips and licked them clean. A bell tolled again—the final warning.

"We need to leave. Now."

"No," I gasped, breathless. "*Please.*"

He released me. I stumbled forward, catching myself with a palm slapped against the mirror, leaving my fingerprints behind. Rixon was already grabbing my arm, pulling me across the room. I barely saw our surroundings, head still spinning, body still screaming.

"I want you hungry for me, Aramina. Hungry and desperate. Behave yourself and I'll reward you."

I gaped, mouth working like a starved fish.

When I next blinked, we were striding through the door. The palace swam back into view. I had minutes to control myself, to regain composure. I would need every bit of it, for what was to come.

CHAPTER 10

RIXON

Rixon adjusted his pants before leading Mina into the palace dining room. It was all wood and gilded pillars, rich tapestries, and beautiful statues. Servants in livery flanked every door, lined the walls, and waited to pull out chairs. His father kept a large table, seating nearly one hundred. There were always seat markers, with elegantly scrawled names on card stock; he remembered from his childhood. The king sat at the head, and no one at the foot. That was his mother's place before she'd died, and presumably, it was never filled. A quick glance confirmed this. There was still a card with her name. Queen Leone Kozma.

His chest seized. Thirty years. For thirty years his father had kept that damn card in place. He swallowed against the building ache in his throat.

He hated the male, yet, he couldn't deny the strange emotion, knowing his father refused to replace his mother. That King Maddox Kozma loved Leone, would never love another the same way. Sure, he'd taken bedmates, but they were just a means to an end.

He led Mina towards the head and exhaled. He found cards with both their names, but he'd half expected to only find his. The games his father played were unpredictable.

People milled about, chatting, but they offered wide-eyed bows and respectful greetings. Whispers echoed in their wake, about his return, about the woman on his arm. Neither he, nor Mina, wore gloves to cover the markings on their hands. He hoped it would irk his father.

Already, more than half the table was occupied. He reached for Mina's chair, not trusting a servant to the job, and scooted her in, taking his own afterward. His father's remained empty, as did the four chairs across from him. Probably for his father's advisors.

"All hale King Kozma!" a voice called. Those already seated rushed to their feet. He scoffed, then stood, taking Mina's hand, helping her with her chair. This was the kind of pomp he hated. So fucking *excessive*. Standing and sitting—sitting and standing.

The king was dressed smartly in a military style uniform. As if he'd seen battle. He strode to his chair and a servant rushed forward to help him settle. Once he was seated, everyone else did the same, stragglers racing to grab theirs before the dining room doors closed.

The chairs across from him were pulled out—

Mina choked, more of a laugh than anything. A moment later, he saw why. "*Fuck me*," he hissed, barely loud enough for her.

Trudy Holland, dressed in an obnoxious mint colored gown, her flaming hair piled atop her head, took a seat across from him. Her father, Diego Holland, took up the chair closest to the king. A third was filled by a younger red-head, near spitting image of Trudy. Gods, *two* of them? Finally the fourth was occupied by a man near his age, also red hair, but his was cropped close. He wore a fine tunic and looked as if everything around him smelled unpleasant.

The man's eyes darted to Rixon's. He merely lifted an eyebrow, staring him down, until the man looked away. A brother, then, most likely. How many fucking Hollands were there? Were they all as obnoxiously annoying as Trudy?

"I take it you don't recognize the brother, either?" Mina teased, leaning over to quietly speak in his ear. He threw her a glare. She merely grinned back.

Oh, he had plans for his lady witch. They were only growing darker—

"Welcome, welcome." The king lifted a hand to speak. Silence fell. Heads leaned around heads as nearly one hundred patrons attempted to get a look at the king. "Tonight's dinner is particularly special. My son has found his way home, at last." His father motioned towards him. A polite round of applause sounded. Rixon didn't clap. Neither did Mina.

Trudy looked as if she might damage her hands, for how hard she beat them together. Was *this* to be his punishment, then? Staring at her across the table for an entire meal? She caught his gaze and smiled. There was something about it that sent alarm bells ringing.

"Now, let's lay on the good news. With Aleksander's return, we may finally begin preparations for another joyous occasion. I believe congratulations are in order for a certain happy couple. Better late than never. Let us all raise a glass to Aleksander Kozma and Trudy Holland. May their marriage be prosperous."

Mina choked. Around the table, drinks lifted into the air. "*Fuuuck*," he hissed, eyes darting towards Trudy, who sat beaming.

"To Aleksander and Trudy," voices echoed, goblets clinking.

His skin flushed hot. A light perspiration broke across his brow. His eyes darted around the room, not quite seeing.

So, *this* was his father's next move? His lips curled, teeth bared. He made to stand, to storm from the room. Mina's hand found his leg, holding him in place. "Breathe," she whispered against his ear. "Just breathe, Rixon."

He tried to rip his leg from her touch. "*You will not react,*" she ordered, pulling on the bond. "*Calm down.*" The force of it, the pull of her words, instantly grounded him. "That's better," she whispered, but she did not release him. Instead, she quickly raised her own goblet and clinked it with the person beside her, drinking her fill. An act. She was playing along.

Jaw clenched, his teeth nearly cracked.

This was what his father wanted—for him to make a scene. Mina was smarter, but at this moment, he didn't care. He fucking *hated* his father.

When he turned, he found the king's gaze on him. A slow, victorious smile stretched across Maddox's lips. "Congratulations on your new bride, Aleksander."

"I don't remember proposing," he said, keeping his voice calm, only because the bond forced him to.

"I proposed on your behalf."

"I see. And when was this decided?"

"Diego is one of my closest advisors. We made plans decades ago, did we not?"

Diego nodded. "Certainly, Your Majesty. Trudy and I, all of the Hollands, are most honored. We cannot wait to join your family."

"Of course you can't," Rixon muttered, his voice deadly calm. Beside him, Mina merely witnessed everything taking place, her eyes calculating.

How the fuck was she so relaxed? He wanted to shake her. To scream at her. *This is what happens!* he wanted to say. *This is why you cannot underestimate him. This is why we never should have come here.* But instead, her leash forced him to remain composed.

And yet…just beneath her facade, he noticed her fury. She hid it well, but he knew her better than anyone. Knew she had pushed it down deep, for the sake of doing what needed to be done.

Her hand against his leg stroked back and forth, trying to calm him. He felt her love through the bond. A quiet sigh left his nose. He needed to trust her. That's what the bond was built on. Trust.

So, he allowed it to control him. He sat through the first course, a tomato and seafood bisque, ate enough to be convincing, and refrained from speaking. Trudy did enough talking for everyone. She still hadn't acknowledged Mina's presence. If she saw Mina as a threat, she didn't make a sign of it. No doubt his father had assured her the witch would soon be out of the picture.

But...*how*? What were his father's next plans? If a betrothal wasn't enough to scare her away—and it certainly wouldn't be —what would he do after?

He stretched his neck, side to side, willing his muscles to relax. He needed to keep his guard up. There was no doubt in his mind that Maddox would kill his witch. He needed to keep that from happening.

The second course arrived, a chopped green salad with a light herb oil dressing. He began to relax, to fall into Mina's control. With his fading anger, common sense swept in. Mina had been right to stop him, to keep him from storming out of the room like a petulant child.

His chest expanded. She'd been *brilliant*. His eyes darted towards her frequently, so beautiful in her blue gown. More lovely than any female at this table, than any female in the kingdom.

Plates were cleared. As the third course arrived, a baked chicken in a light cream sauce with rice, he was fighting an urge to reach for her. His fingers itched. He held himself together, picking at his food. Soon enough, his hand found her leg, fingers bunching against the fabric of her skirts. He fisted them, continuing to eat. She made no acknowledgment of his movements. Not until he began to draw her skirt up along her leg, hidden beneath the tablecloth. Her eyes darted towards his—a warning. He slipped his fingers along the inside of her thigh, then found the apex of her thighs. She gasped. It was a tiny sound, unnoticed over the din of conversation, save for his own ears.

He looked sidelong at her. The warning in her gaze wasn't enough to deter him. He slipped his middle finger inside her, noticed from the corner of his eye the way her hand faltered, fork coming to rest on her plate, the way her eyes took on a far away look. She squeezed her thighs against his hand.

He curled his finger once, twice, then slipped it free, pulling away from her. Her cheeks were flushed. But she mastered herself. Not a single hint of black. She'd gotten very, very good at control over the past few weeks.

Dessert was brought forth, slices of apple pie. He took several bites before leaning back. Across the table, Trudy was tapering down from her discussion of wedding gowns. She'd been talking in a high pitched, squeal to her sister the entire meal, while her father and the king engaged in some odious matter of rice trade.

The king pushed his plate away, then leaned back and turned to him. "Aleksander, you may come by my council chambers tomorrow, along with Lord Holland. We can begin discussing plans for your upcoming nuptials."

"Afraid I'll be—"

"Rixon would be more than happy to join you, Your Majesty," Mina cut in, her hand finding his leg, squeezing. *Play along*, the gesture said. Well fuck, that was the last thing he wanted to do. But instead, he gave a jerk of a nod.

"Very good," his father said.

Mina gave a sweet, innocent smile. She might be orchestrating this, but he had a mind to punish her for it, for subjecting him to so much as a *shred* of his father's diabolical plans.

A few minutes later, dessert plates were cleared and drinks were poured, coffee for some, stronger beverages for others. He and Mina both took coffee. They had a long night ahead of them, if they intended to leave the palace and search for demons, for answers.

Rixon took Mina's hand, striding from the dining room. He'd had to fend off not one, not two, but *seven* separate interruptions on his attempt to flee. Mina, as smooth as she was, handled many conversations for him, much to the disdain of those around him.

What they'd learned that morning, from the other witches, proved all too true here. The king had found a way to make the witches of the Citadel look bad. Pair that with the fact that nobility looked down on anyone that wasn't them, and it was a cocktail for scorn.

"Fucking *finally*," he hissed as the lamp-lit corridors swallowed them up. He was itching to get free. Itching for more than that, too.

"You need to get yourself under control, Rixon," Mina hissed as they emerged into a deserted corridor. He faltered, but didn't break stride. "I know you hate your father, but we have a job to do, and if you rise to the bait, you give him exactly what he wants. Bite your tongue and comply, until we do what we came here to do. Understand?"

"So, that's it? You're okay with this? What he did?" A needle of anger pierced him.

"You think I am okay with the thought of you promised to another?"

"You seemed fine when the announcement was made."

She rounded on him, all but shouting as she said, "I wasn't fine —!" She stopped herself, took a deep breath, and mastered her emotions. "I was furious. But I also know he's playing his games and I'm playing mine. Let him think he has us. It will make things much easier for us. If you think I'll let him take you from me, then you haven't been paying attention. *You. Are. Mine.*" Her nostrils flared. "So—get yourself together. Control your emotions. Don't slip up again or all of this could come crashing down upon our heads."

He looked down at her. Something coiled deep inside of him, a sudden need for control. "Is that all, Lady Witch? Have you any *other* instructions?"

"No. That about covers it." She lifted a brow in challenge, as if waiting for him to argue. He clenched his jaw, glanced around, then dragged her down a side corridor.

"Rix, *what—*"

He pressed her into a shadowed alcove, claiming her mouth, cutting off any further words. Something about the way she scolded him both grated and stoked him in equal measure, inciting a need to possess her. His hands found her hair, wrenched her head back until he had full access. His tongue swept in, tasting her. Their mouths fought—a battle of wills. When he pulled away, his breath was rough. "I'm going to fucking *ravage* you," he promised, speaking against her lips. Then he moved along her jaw.

"Not, not here, Rix," she gasped, trying to push him away.

He ignored that.

Movements frenzied, he dragged her skirts up to her thighs, hoisting her up, wrapping her legs around his waist. She opened her mouth to argue—he claimed it before she could speak. He pressed his cock against her hot center, grinding his hips into her. She groaned against his mouth and he swallowed the sound.

"We...we shouldn't..." she managed, when he pulled away to breathe. But she was already gripping his neck with her fingers.

"No?" He slipped a hand around her thigh, found her wet folds with his fingers, slid inside. She gasped. "I thought I'd left you *aching*, Lady Witch."

"You...you..." Her eyes fluttered closed. In the dim light, the nearby wall sconces cast dancing shadows across her skin, made monstrous by the giant statue partially blocking them from view.

"I told you I'd fuck you in this dress, Mina, but you'll have to be ever so quiet, hmm? Can you do that, little demon? I know it's going to feel good. I know you're going to want to scream, but not this time. You make a sound, I stop. Understand."

"I...I..." The vein in her neck jumped. She nodded. Already, the blackness was spreading from her eyes, little dark veins like lace, trailing outward from her eyes.

A chill raced down his spine, making him hungrier for her. More desperate. He needed her *now*.

Pulling at the ties of his pants, he freed his cock, pressing the head against her slit. Then, with a punishing sweep, he buried himself to the hilt.

She cried out. He pressed his palm to her mouth. There had been a time this had terrified her. Now, her eyes only darkened further.

"Behave," he warned. She nodded, so he removed his hand. Then he began to pump into her, pressed against the wall, her legs wrapped tight, knees jutting to the side, bare now that her skirts were hiked around her waist.

He reached down, gripping her bottom with both hands, pressing his fingers into her generous flesh. Her breaths came faster and faster. He worked his hips, caring little for the obscene sound of flesh slapping flesh—

Voices made him hesitate.

"Rixon," she gasped, trying to get him to stop before discovery. But he couldn't end this. Not now. Already, her walls were fluttering around him, squeezing like a vice.

"Stay quiet," he warned, pressing in closer into the shadows.

His cock hardened, each thrust sending a lick of pleasure surging through him. Something about the thrill of being spotted made him more desperate. The voices moved closer—

Mina moaned, "Gods, yes!"

The voices faltered, then gasped. He didn't turn, didn't acknowledge their presence at the alcove's mouth, watching him fuck his way to oblivion. A few utterances of shock followed.

He drove his hips harder, surging into Mina.

"Unbelievable," one of the voices hissed, before finally moving off. They'd lingered, though, and watched the two shadowy figures slaking their thirst upon one another.

Mina's chest rose and fell in bursts, her flushed skin unmistakable. "Good girl," he crooned, then ground his hips into her. She gasped. Her orgasm swept in and claimed him, decimating him. He followed, pumping into her, filling her, until all that was left were the sounds of their ragged breathing filling the corridor.

CHAPTER 11

MINA

My footsteps pounded on the cobbles, mingling with my racing pulse, filling my ears with a roar. Each of my breaths came in splintered gasps, my side burning worse the heavier I breathed. I'd never needed to run as a witch, never needed to chase down my quarries. As part of my training in the Citadel, we'd faced demons in mock-trials, in close circles, always contained. Physical activities, like brute fighting, had been left to the wielders.

We'd exercised our minds, not our bodies.

"Running through city streets was *not* what I signed up for," I cried as Rixon and I rounded a corner. I felt the demons, not far ahead. They were stationary, and I dreaded the reason.

"If you're already out of breath, Lady Witch, I'm not working you hard enough."

My laugh was strained.

We rounded another corner. The pull brought me closer. I'd felt it spring up five minutes ago. We'd been keeping to the shadows, patrolling, when the intense pressure jerked me in this direction.

"Damn it!" I swore.

Screams met my ears. Light spilled into the street from an open doorway. Splintered wood scattered the entry. The demons had broken through. "Fuck," I cried, not bothering with caution as I crossed the threshold. Immediate relief surged through me.

Only a single demon.

My eyes darted over everything. A male stood in a billowing nightshirt wielding a glowing fire poker in one hand, and a Nebrine dagger in the other. His nightshirt was stained with blood, his breathing labored.

The Kollm was small for a demon. Its shrunken head with sunken eye sockets where eyes ought to go, if it had any, gnashed at the open air, hissing each time the man caught it with the fire poker—

A whimper pulled my gaze across the room. Cloistered in the pantry near the kitchen were several small faces. A female stood just outside the door, kitchen knife in hand. Her face was pale, eyes wide. The blade in her hand trembled.

A mother ready to defend her children.

I cataloged everything in an instant as Rixon rushed in, sword at the ready. He sprinted across the room, sweeping his blade in a killing arc. The head was severed off the Kollm in a single blink. It dropped. Before it rolled more than once, I incinerated the body, careful not to burn anything.

The children were already traumatized. They didn't need to see more than they had. Even still, they'd have nightmares.

The female cried out and ran for the male, throwing her arms around him. The children tentatively stepped from their hiding place. Rixon went to them. My heart burst as he sank to his knees and began speaking in hushed whispers—two young girls, no older than five, and a young boy, perhaps six or seven. The boy nodded, then took his sisters by the hand and led them away, Rixon at his heels, as they passed through a doorway. It led to their bedroom.

"Let me see to your injuries," I told their father. His eyes widened and he stepped away, wary of me. "Please, I won't hurt you."

His throat bobbed. At last, he allowed me to lead him to a chair. I crouched down and began. Each wound brought a hiss of pain, until his forehead was beaded with sweat, his breathing heavy.

"What are your names," I asked while I worked, trying to distract him.

"Finnigan," he managed. "Fin, for short. And my wife, Karla."

"Pleased to meet you. Though, I wish we were meeting under better circumstances." I poured my magic into the gash along his bicep. "And your children?"

"Connor, Sarafina, and Zara."

"Those are beautiful names," I mused as I took his hand and knitted together the skin along the back of his wrist.

He hissed. "Does it always hurt so damn much, Lady Witch?"

"Always," I assured him, then chuckled. "If it helps, I've had grown males—*wielders*—cry while I do it."

"Yours?"

"Even mine." A small smile pulled at my mouth. I heard Rixon snort from behind me. "But to be fair, he was nearly dead. I think he cried more for the situation than my healing touch. I will save you from the particulars."

My mind jumped back to that day, when I had nearly lost him. The decision I'd made to save him had changed everything. There were a few points in my life, pivotal moments, like when I'd gained my magic and destroyed my sister in the process, that stood stark against the rest. Healing Rixon with a kernel of demon power was another of those.

Fin nodded, assuaged. Still, I didn't miss the way he tried even harder to clamp down on his pain after that. As if he was determined to do better than even some of the bravest. I admired that.

His wife stood behind him, her hand on the top of his head, fingers brushing through his hair.

"There, all done," I said.

He sank back into his chair. I rose to my feet, resisting the urge to groan at the ache in my body. Fatigue, not from magic, but from a long night.

"You did well tonight," I said to them. "Very few survive a demon attack without proper training."

Fin seemed to puff up even bigger.

"Lady Witch?" Karla asked . She had sandy colored hair, her face riddled with fine lines, laugh lines from a happy life. She moved around her husband and held forward a coin pouch. "For your services. For saving our lives."

"No," I said, shaking my head, closing her fingers over the pouch. "I will not accept payment for this. It was my duty, and if anyone pays me, it ought to be your king."

She blinked. "You're sure?"

"Positive."

One look about their home told me enough—that they weren't well off. They had mouths to feed. I would never accept their money.

At last, she nodded then shuffled away with the pouch. Rixon spent a few minutes speaking with Fin about the door. Then we bid them goodnight and emerged back out onto the street.

After a few steps, Rixon pulled me into the darkness of an alley and pushed me against a wall. "I *cried*? Lady Witch? Really?"

I clamped down on my smile. "Well, to be fair, you balled your eyes out like a baby, but I figured you didn't want me sharing *that* much."

"*You little demon*," he hissed, then brought his mouth to mine, stealing a quick kiss. "I was *crying*," he explained, pulling away to look at me, "because I couldn't lose you—couldn't bear a world without you in it."

"As I said to Fin—*particulars*."

He snorted, then pressed his body against mine, his knee slipping in between my legs, thigh pressing against my apex.

"Rixon!" I scolded. It was the middle of the night, and we'd just fought off a demon. A seedy alley was the last place I wanted his arousal.

"Just need you to feel what you do to me, Lady Witch." Then he nipped at my bottom lip, stepped away, and adjusted his pants.

We stood upon a rooftop, gazing out over the city. I waited for the familiar pull that signaled more demons, keeping my cloak tight around me, despite the temperate air. It felt safer, as if I could ward off whatever was happening in Corinna.

My mind continued to jump back to Fin's family until a hard scowl marred my features. They could have died tonight. Others already had. How many demons had broken into homes? How many losses had Corinna seen?

The king forced our witches indoors under threat of arrest should they break the curfew. Why? To tarnish our reputation?

My lips flattened. "He's letting innocent people die," I spat. "I want to know where they're coming from. How they're getting inside the city."

"As do I, Lady Witch."

"I think I have an idea on how to accomplish it."

"Oh?" That got his attention.

I rubbed the back of my neck, knowing he wouldn't like this. "It will require me to use my magic—not my witch magic, my demon magic."

I hadn't planned for it, that day. Hadn't planned to absorb all that power. But I'd been distracted by the blade piercing my body. I'd accidentally lost my hold on it, and it had rushed right into me, sweeping through me. Just another of those pivotal moments that had changed my life.

Ever since that day, my abilities had multiplied. I could do more than see in the darkness; I could communicate with them. I'd only done it once, that day Rixon and I had a picnic on the river outside Rockfall. I hadn't tested the boundaries yet, too afraid by what I'd find.

"You want to...you want to ask a *demon*?" he said, failing to hide his disapproval. "And you're just going to...what? Walk up to one and go, 'Oh, hello, demon. What are you doing in the city? And where did you come from?' Because that sounds like a grand plan, Mina."

So many words.

"Thank you, Lord Wielder, for your excellent sarcasm. And yes, it is a grand plan."

"No. Absolutely not."

"I will do whatever it takes to get to the bottom of this."

"And if the demon leads you to the witches?"

"Then we'll know they're the ones behind this—that they betrayed us. But at least we'll have an answer."

"Fuck me," he muttered, scrubbing a hand over his face. He looked tired, more tired than I'd seen him. Being here, in this city, was taking its toll.

I went to him and took hold of his arms, circling my fingers around his wrists. "Look at me, Rixon," I said, voice softening. "I love you, you know that? I love you very much. But you're being a pain in my ass right now. We need to do this. I don't want to be in your awful father's presence any longer, especially now that there's this gods awful impending betrothal hanging over us. And neither do you, unless..."

"Unless, what?" he demanded, lifting his brows.

"Unless you'd like to stay and make Trudy your wife?" I challenged him with my gaze.

He growled. "Careful, Lady Witch. I *will* bend you over this ledge and I will fuck you for the entire city to hear, if you don't mind your sass."

I grinned, letting a bit of darkness seep into my eyes.

"Insufferable woman," Rixon muttered. I mock pouted. "Kiss me," he ordered, voice dropping low. So I did, lifting onto my toes to reach his mouth, releasing his wrists to wrap my fingers in his silky hair.

When I stepped back, I studied his face, turning serious. "You want to talk about it? About the betrothal?"

Aside from my scolding him earlier, after dinner, and our reckless fuck in the corridor, we hadn't said all that much about what had happened.

"Not really."

"But..."

"No, Lady Witch."

"All right." I'd give him his space. I respected his wishes. "But when you're ready, I'm here."

———————————

I smoothed the formal tunic over Rixon's broad chest, relishing in the bulge of his muscles beneath my fingertips. "Now," I said, "Play nice, and be compliant. Go along with everything your father says and *behave* yourself." I threw last night's words back in his face. Even now, I couldn't stop replaying the way he'd taken me against the alcove wall, the fire in my chest, the way his recklessness made my insides purr.

Gods, I'd become a wonton little hussy.

"Not sure I'll manage that." He glanced down at himself, frowning.

"Rixon..." I warned. He shrugged. "Would you like to go in under my control?"

It was meant as a joke, but—

"Yes, I think that would be best."

"You...you're serious?" My brows drew together. "You want me to use the bond to force you to comply with your father?"

"If you don't, I'm going to do something I'll regret. I'll probably break his fucking nose, at the least."

I sighed. "Rixy, what am I going to do with you?"

"Don't call me that," he barked, irritated.

"No? But Rixy's so cute."

"Gods, Mina! *Miny*? There. How about that?"

"It sounds like *Meany*." I pouted.

"Well?"

"All right," I huffed. "Point taken." I loved this man—so very much. "Rixon, you have better control than anyone I've ever met, except perhaps Herrin."

"I have better control than Herrin."

"And still, you'll bash your father's face in the second he says something insulting."

"Exactly."

I regarded him. "He only does it to rile you. And you let him."

"Perhaps you don't fully understand the extent of his rearing."

A lump formed in my throat. "I don't—I am not sure I ever will. I was raised by loving parents, Rix. I wish you had been too. Speaking of...when am I going to meet your *other* mother? Coralayne?" I batted my eyelashes, teasing.

"Fuck," he muttered, rubbing the back of his neck. He'd forgotten, in this blur of court drama, he'd completely forgotten about his wet nurse—Jessin's mother.

"We can go this afternoon, after you're finished with your *courtly duties*," I suggested. He nodded. "Now, are you certain you want my control for this?"

"Yes."

I sighed, then gave him the order, phrasing it so he wouldn't misbehave. He finished preparing, making sure his attire was *just so*, and then I saw him off. I waited until he was gone before slipping out of his room and finding my own way through the palace. I wasn't sure where I was going, content to explore, to follow corridors, check unlocked doors, and span staircases. Most of the palace was occupied by servants—no small surprise, since it required an army to keep a place like this clean—rushing about with arms full of linens, baskets of brushes and other cleaners, carpentry tools, and more.

I wandered until my feet took me all the way to the top of a tower. A staircase spat me out on a flat roof where I looked out over the city. Here, I could see all the way to the sea. That the morning fog and overcast clouds had cleared up. Overhead, gulls and other sea birds swooped and cawed, calling out to one another.

What's happening to you? I wondered, wishing the city below could simply tell me the answer.

My eyes lingered on the shipping yards, where we'd been earlier. Even at this distance, the cranes were obnoxiously large, ever in motion. Rixon had told me that the workers kept long hours, often late into the night, until it got too dark and their lanterns made the work too hazardous.

It was peaceful up here, removed from the chaos below; I could almost believe that bad things weren't happening, that people weren't dying. I shut my eyes, inhaling deep. In my chest, the constant pressure I'd felt thrummed with the pace of my heart.

What *was* it? I hadn't voiced my worry to Rixon. Hadn't wanted to add to his burdens. But...I was afraid.

It reminded me of the same pressure I'd felt near the rift. So similar...and yet, it wasn't exactly the same. I pressed my sternum with both my palms, one over the other, as if pushing against myself might ease it—

The hairs on the back of my neck lifted. I had the immediate sensation of being watched. As if someone or something lurked just behind me.

I whirled and caught sight of a large, dark blur in my periphery. Heart fluttering, I searched. The roof was empty, silent except for the faint sound of flapping wings.

No—it was just my imagination.

I took a deep breath and let it out in a loud rush. It was a left-over from my nightmares. From the flapping wings in my dreams each night when I fell asleep. I turned back to the city, spread below me in blocky levels.

"The king has been very naughty..." said a voice in my mind, but not my voice.

I screeched and spun in a full circle, eyes darting over the empty stones behind me, then up at the sky. Nothing.

My breath hitched. I looked towards the door on the roof and considered bolting for safety. But...

It was the same voice—I'd heard it a few times in my dreams, too. Broken fragments. Leftovers.

"Get out of my head!" I hissed, rubbing my temples.

The only answer was a dark, rumbling laugh, fading, fading, fading into nothing. My gaze darted over every segment of the palace rooftop, every level, every exposed window. There was no sign of it. No sign of the demon that felt more a part of my imagination than ever.

Sometimes, if I tried hard enough, I could convince myself that I'd been mistaken. I'd been mistaken that day I'd seen it emerge from the rift. It had happened so quickly, and I'd been under immense duress. If I tried hard enough, I could convince myself that it was entirely my imagination. That this was the price of the thing festering inside me.

"With blood we shed... With blood we keep..."

I shivered, turning on my heel, retreating. I reached for the door and threw myself over the threshold, back into the dimness of the palace.

"With blood we guard the blackness deep..." The words repeated, an echo in my mind. *"With blood...with blood..."*

I took the stairs two at a time, then strode through the place, trying to escape the words. When I found my way back to Rixon's room, I slammed the door behind me, leaning against it, breathing hard. Only then did the chanting end. Only then did my mind become my own, once more.

CHAPTER 12

RIXON

Rixon gritted his teeth and kept his mouth closed, nodding only when prompted. Somehow, his compliance dragged him through the next hour and a half in his father's company. A wedding date was set, some four weeks from today. It was decided that Rixon and Trudy would preside over the particulars of the wedding. Dowry was discussed. Title conferment assured. And...that was that.

Mina's control had been useful for the first twenty minutes, when he wanted to shove a knife through his father's eye sockets. After that, he resigned himself to indifference, tuning out the majority of it. He'd spoken a couple of one word responses, but could not be bothered for more.

The moment chairs began scraping, he was on his feet, eager to leave. Lord Holland exited with the king's steward as he made for the door. He was nearly free of the king's clutches when his father said, "Glad you saw fit to behave yourself today, *boy*."

His shoulders tightened. He sighed, turned. The expression on his father's face was one of suspicion, with narrowed eyes and a clenched jaw. He ignored that and said, "Father, I haven't been a boy for a long while."

"In my eyes, you're a boy until you start acting like a man. You can begin by freeing yourself of that wretched witch. You have obligations here. Leave the Citadel to their own."

His skin prickled with heat. A number of choice words filtered through his mind, but none could be spoken with Mina's leash firmly in place. And yet, he couldn't just turn and walk away.

"Tell me, *Your Majesty*, what could be more important than protecting the kingdom from demons?" he bit out, forced to keep his voice calm, pleasant.

"Nothing. *Nothing* is more important." King Kozma's thumb rubbed at the inside of his right palm, against the fabric of his black gloves, eyes momentarily distant.

Rixon snorted. "And yet, you sit in a fancy chair all day and make pronouncements."

His father's lips curled, gaze turning cold. When he next spoke, his voice was weighted. "You think that as a ruler, I do not protect my people? That as the ruler of this country, I do not make sacrifices daily?" The king's hands dropped to his sides.

Rixon's eyes snagged on the motion. He gave his head a subtle shake, as if to clear his thoughts. "I'm done having this conversation, Father." Without being granted dismissal, he turned on his heel and strode from the council chamber.

He walked swiftly, fists clenched at his sides. Those he passed bowed, but he didn't notice. How *dare* his father dictate his future?! The king acknowledged the importance of protecting the kingdom, and yet, believed Rixon's time was better spent elsewhere. There was nothing more noble than the work he was doing, keeping people safe. He thought back over all he and Mina had accomplished together. A far cry more than his father, who sat on his golden throne, squabbling with nobles, issuing tax hikes, eating fine food, hosting parties, taking advice from his multitude of advisors.

Sacrifices?! What a farce!

By the time he reached his quarters, he felt the scowl on his face like an ache. Sighing, he took a deep breath then went inside. Mina sat on the couch, but she jumped to her feet when she saw him.

"You're back."

Something was wrong. He strode to her, taking her chin in his fingers, tilting her face toward the light. "What's the matter? Why are you so pale?"

"I...I'm not pale. I'm fine. I just spent some time exploring the palace, that's all."

He hesitated, searching her eyes. "Someone give you trouble?"

"No. Just..." She pulled her chin free and rubbed her temple with the inside of her wrist. "I..."

His shoulders relaxed and he placed his hands on her arms, rubbing up and down, soothing. "Mina...since when do you keep secrets from me? I thought we were past that?"

Never mind that he'd been closed off these past few weeks.

"I...it's nothing. Really. Just whatever is inside me. Sometimes it's a lot."

"Has something changed? Is it hurting you?"

"No. No, nothing like that. Really, it's nothing. But...I'll let you know if anything changes. I promise." Despite the way she smoothed her expression, he saw remnants of fear in her eyes.

He inhaled, willing himself to drop it. She'd come to him when she was ready. He needed to give her the space she was giving him. Space to deal with whatever was troubling her.

Speaking of space...

"Shall we go and meet Jessin's mother?"

The offer was another step towards acquainting her with his past. But like the other concessions he'd made, this was also shrouded in happy memories, making it easier to share.

"Oh, yes. I'd love that."

He tilted her chin and kissed her sweetly. Her exhale tickled his skin, breath mingling with his. Then he led her from the palace.

Coralayne lived in a comfortable townhouse a few blocks from the palace. It had taken several inquiries to track her down, but they'd found her home easily enough. Rixon smiled when he caught sight of her in the small garden, hunched over, weeding.

Her black hair was streaked through with silver, and she'd put on a little weight as she'd grown older, no longer chasing two rambunctious children. He took a deep, steadying breath, just outside the little gate. "Cora?"

Her head snapped up. The years had been kind to her. She was pretty as ever, with laugh lines framing her eyes, and narrow, almost unnoticeable wrinkles along her forehead.

Her eyes narrowed, then widened. She surged to her feet, whipping soiled hands on her thick skirt. "Aleksander? Is...is that you?"

"Hi Nona." It was a name he'd called her as a child, one he'd grown out of.

Her surprise softened, but her eyes narrowed. "If you think Nona-ing me is going to chase away my anger at you for leaving without a goodbye, then keep dreaming, child." Heat crawled up his neck.

She strode to the gate and unlatched it, lifting her hand, placing it against his cheek. It smelled of earth, and he didn't care that it still bore remnants of her gardening. For a long time, she'd been taller than him, but then he'd shot up like a weed. Now, he stood nearly a foot taller.

A small huff escaped her lips. "I always knew you'd be handsome, and you are, even with these scars marring your strong face. What happened to your nose, child? I hope you gave the bastard a good strike in return."

"A demon, and yes, chopped its head off."

"Well then." She nodded. "Good. Now," she dropped her hand and turned to his witch, "let me get a look at *you*."

Mina stepped forward, hesitant, and Cora took her hands, looking her over. "Pretty thing, aren't you? With intelligent eyes. Yes. Good. Aleksander has done well for himself."

"It's a pleasure to finally meet you, Coralayne. Rixon *and* Jessin told me a lot about you. They both speak of you fondly."

"They do, do they?" Cora threw Rixon a suspicious look, giving Mina's hands a squeeze before dropping them and stepping back. "Well, they'd better. I only spent half my life trying to teach 'em to be good boys, or, one of them anyway, since the other ran off."

"You know I didn't have a ch—"

"Oh, be quiet. I know all about it. Now, come in off the street. I'll make us some tea."

Cora turned and led them indoors. He immediately took to analyzing her home. It was several levels, shared with other town homes along the block, each with its own gated garden out front. The sitting room was warmly furnished, with plush white sofas and gold pillows. There were a few paintings on the wall, and a portrait of Jessin in his military uniform. Mina gravitated towards it, a small smile spreading across her lips.

"He's a handsome boy," Cora mused from the doorway into the kitchen. "Too handsome for his own good, I'd say. Doesn't want to settle down. Doesn't want to get married. But he takes good care of his mother. So I leave him to his diversions."

"He's very handsome, indeed. Though," Mina spun around, her eyes flashing toward Rixon. "Not as handsome as my Rixon."

Cora barked a laugh. "Rixon, hmm? I heard the rumors yesterday. Oh, yes. Also heard that father of yours announced your betrothal to Trudy Holland. But, we can discuss it in a moment. Settle yourselves. I'll grab tea."

They found seats beside each other. A few minutes later, Cora was bustling in with a tea tray and cakes. Silence fell, only the sound of little spoons clanking on porcelain before they sat back sipping. "Now," Cora said, "tell me everything."

Rixon snorted, but he did exactly that. He told her of how he'd gone to the Citadel after running away. Got paired with a witch, Ena, who later died. He left out all the details about his abuse. How he'd gone back to the Citadel, for fear of having nowhere else to go, and had found Mina.

At that, he reached for her hand, lacing their fingers together, rubbing his thumb over her skin. Cora didn't miss the motion. "I think I'm the luckier one," he finished. "But my Mina will insist otherwise."

"And what of *you*, girl?" Cora asked. "What's *your* story?"

Mina launched into an abridged tale of her past, where she'd come from, what had happened to her family, and how she'd trained in the Citadel. He listened to her talk, watching her. With each word, his chest swelled.

"She's the strongest witch the Citadel has seen for a long, long time," he blurted, unable to help himself. Nor could he help the huge smile that bared his teeth.

"I would have expected nothing less, from a woman who snared my Aleksander," Cora said, fondly. "The two of you love each other, then?"

"Very much," they both said at the same time, glancing at each other.

Cora snorted. "Well, you've my blessing then. Not that it counts for anything round these parts."

"Counts a lot for me," he found himself saying.

"It counts where it matters," Mina added.

"And your father? I bet he's not too keen on the matter?"

Mina snorted. "If you mean promising him to another and planning a wedding counts as *not too keen*, then yes, I'll say."

"But you won't be going through with it, of course." Cora's statement wasn't a question.

"I hope to have us far, far away from here by then. But only after we've sorted things out."

"The demons," Cora said, nodding. "They started popping up not too long ago. The curfew came about a few days later. Whole city's been locked down since then." Cora drained her teacup and set it on the tray. "No one knows what's going on, or why the witches let it happen."

"Who says it's the witches?" Mina hedged.

Cora shrugged. "They're the ones letting it happen—or, so everyone says."

"And what do *you* believe?" Rixon asked.

"Not sure at this point. But what I *do* know is people are dying, Aleksander, and there are six witches in this city who seem to be letting it happen."

"I'm not sure the witches have anything to do with it," Mina said. Cora lifted a brow. "Not *entirely* sure," she amended. "The curfew starts at dusk, and the witches must adhere to it." Mina didn't voice their suspicion—that it could be the witches summoning the demons in the first place.

Cora hummed.

"Whatever's going on, I intend to get to the bottom of it," Mina added, throwing a glance in Rixon's direction. He nodded.

They spent more time chatting about milder matters. Cora told them about her life over the past fifteen years, after Rixon had left. When Jessin was old enough, he enlisted in the military, and used some of his earnings to give his mother a comfortable life.

"The king wasn't too happy after you disappeared. I lost my job, and he didn't bother setting me up with anything," Cora explained.

Rixon's throat started to ache. He dropped his gaze. "I never thought about what my leaving might mean for you—"

"Oh, stop that." Cora raised her hand. "You did what you had to, and I'm not bitter about it. If anyone's to blame, it's your father."

Regardless of her words, he couldn't help the heat that flushed his skin. The shame he felt over abandoning the only woman who'd been a mother to him. "I'm sorry, Nona."

"Don't be. I'm comfortable. It was a bit rough, starting out anew, leaving the palace behind and settling in the city. But, Jessin helped."

"Were...were you not noble born?" Mina asked.

"Oh, no dear. Commoner through and through."

"Oh." Mina's brows rose.

"When the king's wife died in childbirth, the call went out for birthing mothers. I was in a hard place, husband dead—killed in a shipping accident at the docks—with no money to make our next rent, no money to eat more than a single meal a day. Jessin was only a couple months old, and I was terrified. So, I answered the call, but I didn't expect nothin' to come of it." Rixon exhaled, leaning back. This was all news to him. He listened silently as Cora continued. "There were a few others who answered, too. The king had his pick from a handful of us, certainly. I was the youngest. And...well...I think my pleasing looks had something to do with it."

"Oh..." Mina said again.

Cora chuckled, waving a dismissive hand. "Don't get the wrong idea, dear. He never touched me *that* way, but if he was going to have a woman nursing and caring for his heir, well, he wanted her to appear pleasing. I also had more proper manners than the other nursing mothers who presented themselves. But, he *did* insist I undergo etiquette training."

Mina snorted out something that sounded a lot like, *"Shallow bastard."*

"King Kozma offered me a place in the palace for both me and my son, contingent on becoming Aleksander's wet nurse. He gave me a fine salary, whatever gowns I needed to look presentable, and I had all the food I could want. He wanted his son healthy, and that meant my milk needed to be, too." Cora lifted her chin, chest out, shoulders back. "I did a fine job of raising this boy, did I not?" she asked Mina, but continued before Mina could answer. "The king thought so too, so he kept me on after I weaned him. And then he kept me even longer, seeing how close Aleksander and Jessin had grown. But..." She hesitated. "I also think he knew it was important for his son to have a mother figure. I was willing to give Aleksander the love he deserved, when the king refused to do the same. He had tutors, yes, scores of them. But, he was also just a boy, with a need to be nurtured. I...I think the king understood that."

Rixon didn't notice his deep frown until he forced his lips into a line. *This* didn't sound like his father at all. "Jessin never told me any of this," he mused.

"Oh, I doubt he could have, seeing as he was none the wiser as a boy. When you ran, the king no longer needed my services. I had money tucked away, enough to subside on for years. Jessin didn't learn the truth for nearly that amount of time. But when he did..." Her face softened. "That boy of mine has a good heart, he does. He insisted on joining the military, working his way up in the ranks, to ensure he made a proper salary, to ensure I was taken care of."

Rixon's heart cinched tight. Jessin had done all that for her, and what had he done? Run away. Left her in a bind. She was as much his mother as she was Jessin's.

"With my remaining funds, and Jess's salary, we were able to purchase this fine house a few years back. I love that boy." She shook her head, seeming to fall into her own thoughts. "But some days, I wonder if he'll be the death of me."

"Is there anything we can do for you while we are here, Cora?" Mina asked.

He winced. That should have been the first question out of his mouth. Trust Mina to think of such things.

"No, no. I'm comfortable, I am. Just don't stay away. Come and see me when you can."

"We will," he found himself saying, while Mina nodded in agreement. "Of course we will."

They chatted for a few minutes longer before bidding her farewell. But they promised to come back and visit as much as possible. He had lost time to make up for.

"You did what you had to do," Mina said to him, keeping her voice low, gripping his hand as they left Cora's home and walked towards *King's Mantle*. He grunted, not wanting to agree. "You did," she insisted. "And she doesn't fault you for it." Still, he didn't respond, kept his jaw tight, peering at the road ahead. "Come now, Rixon, would she want you to feel guilty?"

"Fuck, woman, you are relentless."

Mina smiled and it was almost contagious. "I'm just saying..."

"Yes, yes. I know what you are saying. And yet, I still feel bad about it. I didn't at the time—a little guilty, yes—but after running into Jessin, and then seeing her again, hearing about what happened."

"That makes sense." She squeezed his hand. "Try not to let it bother you," she added. He nodded, knowing it would be easier said than done. A few minutes later, the inn came into view and not a moment too soon. His stomach growled with hunger, and curfew was nearly upon them.

CHAPTER 13

MINA

The dining room at *King's Mantle* glowed with warmth. Cutlery clanked and conversation buzzed, the sounds weaving together harmoniously. The room was filled with glorious smells as dinner was served. Tonight, it was honeyed buns, a white fish in a rich cream gravy with rice, and sautéed green beans.

All the tables were full, and we'd pulled ours together. It seated all fourteen of us. With the curfew falling, there weren't any visitors besides us, just the patrons staying within the inn.

I hadn't stopped smiling. It was cozy, inviting...*fun*. Because we were surrounded by so many others, we kept conversation light and avoided discussion of demons and the Citadel. Most of it was centered around gossip circulating the city. Rixon hadn't said a word yet, and I was content to let the others do most of the talking.

It wasn't as if the other wielders spoke much either, in the presence of witches.

Anne and Elianna sat on my right side, their wielders across from them, and Rixon on my left. Curiosity had my gaze bouncing between them. I hadn't seen any show of affection between them, not how Rixon and I were. But they did seem companionably comfortable.

Anne asked me about my gowns, "Have they been delivered yet?"

"Just a couple of premade options," I explained.

They also asked how dinner the previous night had gone. My groan said enough. "You will never believe what happened." They were shocked when I told them about Rixon's betrothal. "The entire table toasted to their happiness, and Rixon nearly stormed from the room."

Rixon's face turned rock hard at my confession, so I bumped my shoulder against his, telling him to relax. It wasn't as if I'd allow him to marry her.

"Trudy Holland? She sounds like one of the ridiculous ones. Never did care much for nobility," Anne said, immediately looking for ways to show her solidarity towards our struggle.

Rixon's hand tightened around his goblet. He was always so tense. I put my hand on his leg, sliding it up, up, up, to the one place I'd get a reaction. He captured my hand, pressing it in place over the bulge in his pants and simultaneously threw me a warning glare. My mouth twitched—a promise for later.

Slowly, the dining room began to clear as patrons went to find cozy spots in the common room around the fire, or retire to their rooms. "Will you be going out tonight?" Mya asked, lowering her voice for the two of us. Her wielder, Flynn, had his arm braced along the back of her chair. Of all the pairs, they seemed to have the most outwardly comfortable relationship. Perhaps age drove them to it. Flynn appeared the quiet sort— then again, all wielders appeared that way in the presence of their witches—and overly watchful of his witch. I hadn't heard him speak, except occasionally to lean in and whisper into Mya's ear.

"We plan to, yes." I didn't dare tell her my plans—that I hoped to track the demons to their source. If the witches were behind this, I wouldn't dare tip her off.

"What about last night?" Mya probed. "Did you find anything?"

I kept my voice low, telling her of the family we'd saved. Everyone at our table leaned a bit closer, eager to hear. "We were lucky that the father had a Nebrine dagger," I explained. "And that it was only a single demon. He was wounded pretty badly, but I patched him up. The children will likely have nightmares for days to come, but hopefully they will recover."

We were lucky; the entire situation could have been a lot worse. The witches agreed, but that didn't necessarily mean anything.

We took our leave. It was already dark, the street illuminated only by the yellow glow spilling out of buildings. "Did you enjoy yourself, Lady Witch?" Rixon asked as we walked back to the palace, his voice tight.

I linked my arm through his and smiled sweetly at him. "You're annoyed with me, aren't you?"

"Not terribly."

"Rixon," I chided. But I liked him annoyed. This way, he'd be more fun when we returned to our room. In fact, perhaps I'd orchestrated the whole thing, just to get him on edge. "You are entirely too tense about this whole Trudy Holland matter," I said, knowing that would only add to his ire. "Relax a little, will you? I have no intention of sharing you."

I was poking a bear. I shouldn't have, but it helped me sort my own feelings about it. If I made light of the matter, perhaps I could convince myself to be less angry over it.

Rixon scoffed, but said, "Yes, Lady Witch."

We returned to the palace gates. Rixon called for the guard, who appeared a moment later, eyes widening at the sight of us. "For...forgive me, Your Highness, but I have orders that I am not to open the gate for anyone after curfew."

"Great. We're not anyone. Now, open this fucking gate," Rixon growled, more colorfully this time. Even *I* was reluctant to ignore an order like that. It was the kind that, in the bedroom, I would have jumped to comply with. The guard knew who he was—had acknowledged it. Now, he merely took a few steps back, gulping. I noticed a couple other gate guards hovering in the shadows.

"Sorry...sorry, Your Highness."

Rixon's jaw flexed. "You let us in after curfew last night."

"That...that was before. New orders came a few minutes ago."

"Rix..." I squeezed his arm to get his attention. "If this order was given a few minutes ago, then it was given by the king for one specific reason."

Rixon squeezed the bridge of his nose. The color of his anger rose to his cheeks. I felt my own, too, surging forward.

The king thought to keep us out. He had insisted we take dinner in the dining room each night. Instead, we'd spent ours with the witches.

Rixon reached the same conclusion. His expression turned thunderous. "Break it down, Lady Witch."

My lips parted. "The...the gate?"

"The gate."

I blinked. "You want me to forcefully break through your father's *gates*?"

"As I said." His shoulders drew back. He flexed his neck from side to side, gaze fixed on the guards.

I hesitated, but only for a moment. Deep inside, something woke up, something I tried so hard to ignore. It started to purr.

"As you wish, *Your Highness*," I taunted, a malicious grin splitting my lips. Tunneling down into the well of my magic, I took stock of it. I'd accrued an immense amount, letting it build over the weeks. It was magnified by something else, too. I noticed it there, nestled beside the bright kernel of my soul, a pulsing reddish blip. It had belonged to a demon once, its magic...its *soul*.

I examined the two magics, something I'd done many times of late. They were twined together, nestled close, like lovers, all tangled limbs and soft caresses. I wasn't sure I could ever break them apart.

I pulled a wisp of my magic free, magnified by the thing that fed it. Using my hand, I sent it surging for the gate. It struck, the sound of it reverberating through the air like a gong. The walls shuddered then grew still. The gates didn't move, didn't budge.

I frowned, taking a closer look. "Rixon, they're made of Nebrine."

"So?"

My breathing turned shallow. It was like a punch to the gut—my realization. "My magic won't work on Nebrine. Not...not anymore."

Still, I tried again, sending another powerful surge. The magic collided with the Nebrine bars, shaking the wall. The Nebrine soaked it up.

Several more guards appeared, drawn to the commotion.

The thing inside me surged. I pulled my hood firmly in place, hiding my face. The king tried to keep me out? *Me*? I would make him regret it.

My vision tunneled, honing in on the guards. They stood, eyes wide, hands resting on their sword hilts. Good, let them fear me. If they refused to open the gate, I would *make* them open it.

I sent my magic straight for them. A different hunger gnawed at my stomach. One eager for flesh—eager to devour. Pulse after pulse slammed against the bars, against the walls, trying to get through—

"Mina..." Rixon pressed his hand to the base of my spine, his touch sending a wave of calm through me.

I blinked. The clawing in my stomach disappeared. My vision cleared.

My hands went limp, falling to my sides. "I...I can't," I quietly said.

A worried frown replaced his angry scowl. He sensed my fear before I buried it. His throat cleared. "We can hunt now, and return at dawn."

"I would have rather *eaten* them," I teased, making my voice sickly sweet. I blinked up at him. Where had *those* words come from? No, never mind, I knew.

Rixon emitted a low growl, setting the little hairs of my arms on end, with shivers racing down my spine—

Ear splitting screeches rent the night air. A sudden, sharp tug pulled at my gut. I whirled out of Rixon's hold, in the direction of the pull. He was at my side in an instant.

"It would seem," I managed, "that we've already got something to hunt."

"After you, Lady Witch." He gestured.

I took off at a sprint.

As a girl, I'd loved running, chasing my father's horses, swallowing up pastures, relishing in the beautiful outdoors, the sunshine. But that had been so long ago. I'd grown lazy in the Citadel, and it showed. That was going to change, here in the capital.

Steadying my breath, I inhaled through my mouth and exhaled through my nose. A curse fell from my lips. I glanced down, taking hold of my skirts to hike them up. I'd dressed up today, which was part of why I'd wanted to return to the palace. Chasing after demons in a beautiful gown *looked* glamorous, but it was hardly practical, and the last thing I wanted was to ruin yards of tulle with demon guts. Too late for that!

More screeches sounded—Trongs, perhaps? And definitely more than one. Last night's experience came racing to the forefront of my mind, the fear on the children's faces. My mouth went dry. What if tonight was worse?

I needed—

"When blood fails, and darkness freed..."

I faltered, almost tripping, and stopped. "What's the matter?" Rixon said, grabbing my elbow to steady me. Wings rustled above me. I looked up but the sky was empty.

"Nothing, we keep moving." I was off again.

Laughter, rich and dark, sounded in the back of my mind. I tried to push it away. To ignore it.

"The price is life..."

The hairs on the back of my neck prickled.

A few blocks later, I found our quarry. Trongs, as suspected. There were four of them. My stomach turned, lifting into my throat. They had something bloodied between them. All that was left was pulp and armor. Guards. The alley was dark.

Trong pincers clicked and clacked, like they were communicating. At my approach, they rounded on me. My arm shot out, stopping Rixon before he could bound forward, sword drawn. "Wait a moment," I hissed.

"Mina they have—"

"I know. But we're already too late." I could not save the guards—what was left of them, but I could get answers.

Nausea swelled in my stomach, twisting. "Stop," I commanded, instinctively pulling on something invisible. The demon kernel inside me? I couldn't be sure. All four demons, with blackened, hunched bodies, and arms like mantises, hesitated. Heads tilted, regarding me.

"What the *fuck*?!" Rixon hissed. Fear clawed down my spine. It was unnatural—*this* was unnatural. Something deep inside me screamed, begging me to reach for my blades, to destroy what stood before us.

I acted against those instincts.

"Where did you come from?" I demanded.

Nothing. Their heads continued to tilt, to regard me. Perhaps they wanted to eat me, but something made them stop, made them hesitate. Something made them question my blood as a witch.

I rephrased my question, my command. "Show me how you got here."

Laugher, again. Dark and oily. *"For blood we have, and blood we give..."*

"Show me!" I commanded again, then gasped, when one of them took a tentative step forward. Then another. And another.

Before I knew it, all four began moving forward, slow, deliberate steps on all fours, pincers clicking.

"Mina," Rixon warned, his voice tight.

I signaled him with my hand to stand down, moving aside, letting the procession of Trongs pass.

Every nerve ending in my body was on edge. I could only watch with wide eyes, my breath staggered. One of the Trongs made a series of clicking noises. A communication of sorts. *Follow*...it seemed to say.

So, we followed.

"I hope you know how this looks," Rixon hissed, voice low.

Yes, I knew exactly how it looked. I was following behind a procession of demons, like some sort of mad demon wrangler. If anyone glanced out their window and saw this, the entire city would be buzzing.

I didn't need to explain myself to Rixon. He was smart enough to know, regardless of how it looked, or how he felt about it. I was here to get a job done.

I half expected them to lead me to the King's Mantle, right into the embrace of the Citadel witches. They didn't, going in the opposite direction. A surge of relief swelled in my chest, not that it meant anything.

The witches, if they were summoning, wouldn't do it at their place of residence. They'd find somewhere else. Somewhere secluded, off the beaten path, where they would go unnoticed.

The demons led us to the docks, to a place along the river. A grate stood, barring a drainage tunnel. It was broken and bent open, as if something had ripped it apart, making it plenty wide for a Trong to pass through.

My stomach dropped.

The Trongs stopped, turning as one to face me. It was eerie. Like they communicated without speech.

"This is where you came from?" I asked. More clicking noises. I peered into the darkness, my skin prickling—

"You there! Halt! In the name of the king!"

"Lady Witch?" Rixon's words were measured. I knew why. If the guards saw us like this...

"Kill them."

Rixon shot forward. I snared the demons in the same moment, and they screeched in fury, perhaps betrayal, but not for long. All four heads rolled seconds later.

The sound of clanking armor was upon us. Four city guards appeared. "What...?" Their eyes darted around before landing on the heap at Rixon's feet. "Are those...?"

"Demons. Freshly slayed. Would you like to dispose of them?" I blinked up at them, offering a sweet smile.

They balked, stepping back several steps.

The one in front shook his head. "No, Lady Witch."

Another guard nudged him, then said, "You are breaking curfew. We are ordered to arrest all who—"

"You would arrest your prince? Your heir?" I asked, infusing my voice with shock. Rixon chose this moment to turn from the carnage. Their eyes fell upon him and widened. They wouldn't dare.

"You know," I added, lifting a brow. "We chased these four through the city, but we found them in an alley beforehand. Can you guess what they were doing?" Silence. "They were eating two of your comrades."

They paled in the darkness.

"There was aught but gore and armor when they finished. We didn't have time to dispose of them—your friends. I'd recommend you head that way, recover what you can, and be happy we are here, else it might have been *you* they came for next."

Their gulps were near audible. One of them had the presence of mind to nod and stammer his thanks.

"You will find them in an alley off Valecross Road," Rixon informed them, his voice low. "Recover what you can."

They turned and fled. I glanced up at him, inhaling. Then I incinerated the bodies and let the ashes sink into the muddy shore. The grate draining into the river was surrounded by mud and ick. With as much grace as I could manage in a gown, I made my way towards it. My boots squelched, sinking and suctioning with each step. I shuddered. *Ick!*

"Marvin is going to be scandalized when he learns what happened to this thing," I muttered. A tiny snort meant Rixon had heard me. I peered inside. The mouth of the hole was dark, ominous.

"It's part of the city's drainage, Lady Witch."

I took a step forward, eager to investigate. Rixon's hand landed on my shoulder, stopping me. "Not so fast. If you're dead set on venturing in there, we will need light. And I go first. Wait here for me."

He waded through the mud and disappeared into one of the dockside warehouses. I waited, but only barely, eager to sniff out whatever the demons had been about to show me. A flap of wings had me glancing over my shoulder. Chills spread across my skin. Had the sound come from the mouth of the drainage?

"With blood we shed, with blood we keep..."

"Stop that," I hissed, sick of the voice. Sick of the taunting ring of it in my head. I'd had enough blood for one night, and certainly didn't need some demon-thing chanting about it.

Rixon reappeared, torch in hand. I squared my shoulders, steeling my nerves. There was no telling what we'd find in this tunnel, and I needed to be ready for it. He stepped past me, and I followed him into the darkness.

CHAPTER 14

RIXON

Rixon entered first, holding the torch aloft, leading the way. His boots sank in the mud, squelching with each step. The smell of muck and decay made his nose crinkle.

"A lot of the sewer tunnels and water runoff goes straight to the river, out to the sea," he explained. Hence, the stench.

Mina kept quiet, one step behind him. "If those stupid guards hadn't come," she grumbled, "we could have used the Trongs to lead us."

He held his tongue, refraining from telling her how chilling it had been to watch her command those demons. He'd seen it before, once, and it had been just as unsettling. It left him on edge.

The tunnel was a mere handspan taller, and just wide enough that if he stretched his arms outward, his fingertips would brush the walls. It was made from a mixture of brick, rock, and earth. There were places that had crumbled with time, where piles of debris littered the ground. Places where water trickled down the walls.

The torch cast dancing shadows as they went. Sometimes there was a flare of moonlight, offered up by a grate overhead. These were just large enough for a body to squeeze through.

They came upon their first junction. Rixon's shoulders tightened. They could continue straight, go left, or right. He studied both directions, lifting the torch high. In those directions, the tunnels were smaller, more ominous.

"Where do you suppose those lead?" Mina mused.

"Probably to different parts of the city. This way should take us further into the heart, towards the palace."

They continued straight.

More branches appeared. Some had a foot or more of water, while others were just mud. And then the main tunnel split; they were forced to pick a direction.

Rixon's muscles coiled tight, ready to spring at the first sight of movement. "Which way, Lady Witch?"

Mina bit her bottom lift, then nodded left. They took the fork, walking along for several tense minutes. It broke in a ninety degree right turn. They followed it, eyes peeled for anything that might give answers.

But...there was nothing.

Besides being the second most unwelcoming place in the city, these tunnels appeared exactly as they ought. There were no summoning stars etched into the mud. No evidence of demons. Nothing.

Rixon slowed to a stop. "I am afraid, Lady Witch, that if we continue any further, we will be lost."

There were the sporadic, overhead grates, but he wasn't sure he wanted to wrestle with them.

Mina sighed, worrying her bottom lip. "The demons led us here."

As if that were enough guarantee to continue. She glanced back the way they'd come. He took a step closer to her.

"Maybe we're off course. Maybe they came from beyond the city. If these tunnels lead to the city's center, surely they spread outward too, past the walls? Beneath them?"

"I suppose it's possible, though improbable."

"What about a rift? Could there be a rift down here somewhere?"

"That's more likely," he said. She chewed on the inside of her cheek, contemplating. "Your call, Lady Witch. Do we continue, or turn back?"

"Is there someone in the city, a master builder or city planner, who might have a map?"

He scrubbed a hand over his face. "Hmm, perhaps. This city was built long ago. If a map exists, it might be hard to find." Her expression tightened into frustration. "We could certainly try," he added.

She nodded. "Then let's turn back. I don't fancy getting lost down here in the middle of the night. This place..." She shuddered. "It gives me the creeps."

He moved closer. "It will be all right," he said, his voice softening, taking her hand, lacing their fingers together. Her eyes, dancing with shadows from the torch, found his face. He leaned down and kissed her forehead, comforting her, then led her back the way they'd come.

Dawn split the sky open with hues of pink and orange. The city was already rich with sounds of the morning. Rixon led Mina from the rooftop where they'd taken up their overnight watch. It was positioned across the street from the *King's Mantle*. To watch the inn in case anyone slipped out during the night.

Not a single person had.

Not until dawn, just as they'd claimed. They emerged in pairs, wielders thumbing their weapons, to sweep through the city and catch any remaining demons, their witches following behind, ready with their magic. All appeared as it ought.

Taking Mina's hand, Rixon led her back towards the palace.

"I'm going to kill your father," she muttered under her breath, scowling as they traipsed up the main thoroughfare.

She was tired and cranky, and they were both filthy. Any minute, the guards would open the portcullis into the palace. He intended to be there the moment that happened.

Not to punish them, even though Mina had wanted that. It wasn't their fault he'd been locked out, out maneuvered by his father. But, the thought certainly crossed his mind.

When they arrived, the palace was open, people already coming and going on business. He ignored everyone, striding through with his shoulders back, looking like hell. He kept a tight hold of Mina's hand.

They tracked a trail of mud through the corridors. It felt mildly satisfying. Though, it was a shame the servants would suffer for it and not his father. The king would never see a single grain of dirt.

They reached his quarters and removed their boots. Mina warded the door, sagging against it when she finished.

"Come, Lady Witch. You are a sight for sore eyes. Let's get you cleaned up." She grumbled something incoherent. He couldn't help the twitch of his lips.

Her midnight black hair was falling free of its bun, wispy tendrils framing her face. She had a few streaks of mud on her neck and cheek. He wished it was something edible, like chocolate, so he might lick it off. Their clothes were dastardly, and would need a thorough wash.

He began undressing her right here, in the entryway. She hummed as his hands lingered over her skin, soothing. When he began on his own clothes, fingers making quick work of the buckles and his weapons, she offered to help. Then he scooped her up and carried her naked body straight into the bath.

Neither had the energy to do more than sit and soak for long minutes until he finally began washing her. "Somehow," she managed, "it always feels a thousand times better when you do it." A huge yawn followed her words. His lungs expanded to their deepest.

He wanted to carry her to their bed, make love to her slowly, languidly, before they both fell asleep. In reality, she wasn't going to last that long. So he made quick work of their clean up, then lifted her from the pool, dried her, and settled her in bed.

A knock sounded, signaling breakfast. He sent the servant away, not wanting to disturb Mina with the wards, then tumbled into bed beside her, drifting off to sleep.

It was only a few hours before a loud pounding beat against his skull. Beside him, Mina groaned, flopping over against him, nuzzling his skin. The pounding continued—someone at his door—before he let loose a string of *fucks* and staggered, naked, to his feet.

"What the fuck do you want?!" he growled at the door, silencing the fist on the other side.

"Forgive me, Your Highness, but your father said to wake you at whatever cost. Council convenes in one hour, and he expects you to be present, as you are his heir, and thus, a member of the council."

"Huh. Is that so? You can tell my father to fuck off." He turned, striding back towards the bed.

"With all due respect, Your Highness," the voice called after him, "he thought you might say that. Said that if you did, he'd have you forcibly removed from the palace, your chambers allotted for another purpose. Your inheritance withdrawn. His words, not mine."

Anger flashed raw and hot, surging through his blood.

Mina appeared beside him, frowning. He rounded on her, trying not to let his irritation get the better of him. "I bet you didn't account for *this*, in your grand plan against my father?"

It was a low blow. This wasn't her fault. Even if she'd made the decision to come here.

Her mouth opened and closed. "I..."

"Well, Your Highness?" The voice was persistent. He wanted to open the door, grab the speaker by the throat. "What shall I tell your father?"

A headache formed between his eyes. He winced, face pinching to ward it off—

"Tell him you'll be there," Mina said, her expression settling. He knew that look. Determination.

Fucking hell. He drew himself up to his full height, crossing his arms. "No."

The refusal surprised even him.

"You *will*," she whisper-hissed, jaw tightening. "This is his game. We are in it for the long haul, Rixon. You *will* be compliant."

His nostrils flared. For the first time, he pushed back. Hard. "I came here to slay demons, Mina," he bit out, "not sit on council meetings like a *fucking prick*."

She took a deep, pained breath, shutting her eyes. When she next looked at him, he saw her guilt. "Please, Rix. I need to buy time so that we can figure this out. Let your father think he has you. For now. Buy me a week—perhaps two. We cannot fight him *and* demons, simultaneously."

"So...you're just giving up then?"

A rapid burst of a laugh broke from her chest. "Hardly. You play along—he thinks he's won. We fix the issue at hand and then disappear. You ran away once, all by yourself. You can do it again, with me." She hesitated, filling the space between him, rubbing her hands along his biceps. He unconsciously reacted, muscles flexing. "Please, Rixi? Do this for us?"

He snorted. "Rixi? Again with that nickname nonsense." And yet, he'd never admit that he kind of liked it.

A dark blush crept up her neck and she shrugged. He inhaled, letting her request sink in. She was right. He knew it, even if he fought against it. They needed to figure out what was happening, and in the mean time, he needed to keep his father off his back. But...what if this was just the beginning? What if his father demanded more, and more, and more?

"Your Highness?" the voice behind the door probed again.

He closed his eyes for a long moment, then lifted his voice and said, "I'll be there."

"Excellent. I'll inform His Majesty. Good day."

"Who *was* that?" Mina asked after the voice departed.

He scoffed. "Definitely not a servant. Not with how they spoke. Probably an advisor, or one of my father's personal assistants." He raked his hands through his hair, still slightly damp. A quick look at the clock told him all he needed to know. "He's doing this on purpose. Shutting me out of the palace for missing dinner, then forcing me to sit in on his council when I've only had a few hours of sleep." He shook his head. "He thinks he can turn me into a prince, into an heir, and punish me when I rebel against it."

Like he was an errant fucking child.

Mina ignored his tirade, instead taking his face in her hands, lowering it to hers, kissing him. It was a slow kiss, thanks for what he'd agreed to. It spoke of pleasure and promise, making his center curl. For a few moments, he forgot about his father, forgot about his responsibilities, forgot about demons... He tasted only her, relishing in the wetness and warmth of her mouth. His cock hardened.

"I'm aching for you," she whispered against his lips, her breath mingling with his. Words used as a weapon of coercion. Not that he needed any coercing. "Come along you my *defiant* wielder, and give me your cock before you go."

A low chuckle built in his throat. "In all my years, I have never met such a needy female."

"Only because no female has ever needed your cock as I have, Rixon."

"Fine, but I'm making love to you this time, and it will be on *my* terms, not yours."

She opened her mouth, but the look he gave silenced any protest. Scooping her up, he carried her to the bed and deposited himself between her legs, devouring her cunt. He lapped and sucked, swiping his tongue in broad, claiming sweeps.

"Rixon!" she gasped out, squirming beneath him, impatient. Always *so* impatient. When she moved *too* much, trying to hasten her orgasm, he growled, pinning her to keep her from it. He would allow her to come when he felt like it, or not at all. His cock turned unbelievably rigid, hardly satisfied as he bucked his hips against the mattress, looking for reprieve.

He could have buried himself in her, could have taken what he wanted, but not this time. No, not after their argument. He would make this slow, torturous for both of them, but especially for her.

He pushed her thighs wider, both hands splayed over her soft skin. He pushed until there was resistance, then gently pushed further, stretching her wide open for him as he feasted. His teeth nipped at the little bud of nerves, ravaging her clit. She cried out, chest rising and falling, nipples pricked towards the canopy overhead. His eyes darted there frequently, watching his effect, relishing in the power it gave him. His witch, helpless against his onslaught, helpless as he took whatever he wanted.

His tongue swirled around her opening, then dove inside. "Rix..." she gasped. "*Please!*" It was a strangled cry.

Even strained, her hips bucked upward, pressing harder against his mouth. He repeated the motion, spearing her. A long, desperate moan built in her throat. She clawed at him, at his shoulders, his neck, his hair, like a wild, feral thing. He felt his skin tear open, vaguely aware that her nails were no longer nails, but sharp claws. Demonic.

That...that was new.

And when he felt a trickle of blood drip down his skin, it only spurred him onward. She wanted to hurt him? He'd take everything and more.

But, he would *not* relent.

Each stroke had her tightening, until that final moment, when he finished her with one, broad sweep, bringing forth a garbled cry. Her hips jerked against him. His center clenched up—desperate—every abdominal muscle straining tight.

He released his hold of her legs, surging upward, over her. Then he slid inside, sheathing himself. He took her into his arms, wrapping himself around her, claiming her. Bare skin to bare skin, every inch of them touching in a lover's embrace. She dug her heels into his back, the pressure against him adding to the ache. Slowly, he slid out to the head, then pressed back into her, pressed *deep*.

"Rixon," she breathed. "That...*yes*! Harder, please."

"No."

Ignoring her demand, he began his languid onslaught, each stroke a deliberate caress within her. She groaned, frustration paired with pleasure lacing her voice. He kept his gaze on hers, eyes darting over her expression, taking in the alluring, black orbs that peered back at him.

"I could make you go faster," she challenged. The voice that spoke was hardly hers. "I can make you do *whatever* I wish."

He caught a glimpse of her teeth. They'd turned to sharp points. Chills skittered down his back. "You could," he challenged, slowing down even further, taunting her. She cried out when he finished a stroke by grinding his pelvis against hers. "But you won't," he added. "Because you owe me this, for what you've asked of me. And because you're a naughty little demon who likes to be punished. Who *deserves* to be punished. Aren't you?"

"I..."

"Say it. Tell me how much you deserve to be punished, *Mina*. Tell me."

"I'm naughty," she managed as he slid out, then pushed back in. Her walls fluttered around him. He froze, mid thrust. "Nooo," she cried out, knowing what he was doing, remembering all too well. Her cunt immediately relaxed around him.

"You deserve to be punished," he prompted, waiting.

"I...I deserve...to be punished." Her dark eyes darted over his. Those words were punctuated by a mew as he surged back into her.

Her tongue flicked out, the motion serpent-esk, giving him another flash of those pointed teeth. She licked along the column of his neck. The wet warmth had his balls tightening painfully. Then a sharp set of needles sent fire up and down his shoulder.

Her teeth sank in deep. Possessive. Claiming.

"Fuck!" He faltered before rolling his hips forward again. She'd bitten him! Her teeth came free, blood following. "You *naughty* little demon," he hissed, twisting his fingers into her hair, tightening his grip into a fist until she cried out. "This what you want, needy little thing? *Pain*? *More*?"

"Yes," she gasped. So he clenched harder, until he pulled the strands tight. Her breaths staggered, her cries becoming pleasure-soaked.

His skin flushed, liquid heat dumping over him.

He tried to slow his motions, tried to hold himself back. He couldn't. Pressing back in, his body took over, betraying him. His movements turned frenzied.

Mina licked up the column of his neck and shoulder, cleaning away his blood. "You dirty little thing," he hissed, knowing exactly what she was doing. "You fucking insatiable female."

She was stealing his fucking control. Her teeth nipped at his neck, the points of her teeth a warning—

The world exploded around him, bursts of color and stars. His body shook, spasming. Mina cried out, her orgasm following, sweeping through her as he emptied himself deep within her. He groaned, riding out each wave, grinding against her clit. Then he slowed, trying to catch his breath.

Fucking fuck.

He tipped his head, finding her face, memorizing the euphoric expression. The demon staring back at him was a happy one. Sated, pleased.

And that? That pleased *him*.

A slow, evil grin stretched across her lips. Her teeth were still pointed. It was sinister. "What was that again, Lord Wielder?" she managed. "What was that about *your* terms?"

He growled, capturing her lips, invading her mouth with his tongue, caring little that the sharp points shredded him.

He claimed her.

When he had the strength to pull away, he did it slowly. She cursed when she noticed the bite. "Do *not* apologize," he warned. He moved to the opposite side of the bed, far enough away that she couldn't heal him. This marked him as hers, and he fucking loved that.

"Wasn't going to," she said, lifting an eyebrow. "I wanted to make you hurt."

"Why is that?" He tried to hide his eager curiosity, and failed.

"Because Trudy Holland thinks she's going to marry you. You belong to *me*, Aleksander Rixon Kozma. You are mine, and no one will take you from me."

Something broke inside him, a dam of relief bursting open. He'd waited to hear this from her, to see more than she'd given him the last time they'd discuss it. To see jealousy instead of calm assuredness.

Fucking finally.

She hesitated, head tilting, then added, "I want to hurt you for that—even if it isn't your fault."

He blinked at her. Just blinked. *Fuck.*

When he tried to speak, he had to swallow first. "I will always be yours, Mina."

Slowly, so very slowly, the blackness in her eyes receded. He caught a flash of something, there and gone. Doubt? Fear? As if the mere thought of him marrying someone else terrified her.

Secretly, he preened knowing that.

He crawled forward, capturing her lips in his. This time, her teeth were blunted. He explored her mouth, then nipped her bottom lip. "I will always be yours," he repeated, pulling away.

Finally, she nodded.

He stood, rising slowly from the bed, eying her. She flopped onto her back, sighing up at the canopy. He struggled to tear his gaze away, to release the sight of her naked and sprawled, the glisten of his seed smearing her inner thighs. He resisted the urge to lean over, to spread it around her cunt, to massage it into her skin.

Instead, he stepped into the bathing room and cleaned himself up. When he stepped out again, he found Mina had cocooned herself beneath the blankets. "You're going back to sleep?" He couldn't decide how to feel about that. Jealous? Slightly. But the sight of her there in his bed had his chest expanding.

"The door is warded against everyone but you and I," she managed through a yawn. "You can come and go without my needing to fuss with it. Enjoy your meeting with your father, Rixon."

"Unbelievable," he muttered, searching for his clothes. He dressed quickly, then went to her, smoothing her hair from her forehead. He drilled into her eyes, searching for the depths of her soul. "I love you, Mina. I love you so very much."

Her expression softened. She bit her lip, then nodded. The look on her face was so fucking open. "I love you too," she whispered.

He rubbed his nose against hers, affectionate, then kissed her on the forehead. There was still a trace of the bond in place, the one that would force him to stay calm and collected around his father. And thank fuck for that, because he was *this close* to finding the courage he needed to kill the asshole. Instead, he took a final look at his sleepy witch. He let the sight of her bolster him, then strode from the room, bracing himself for the day ahead.

Chapter 15

Mina

The library smelled exactly as it ought to. I turned in place, eyes trained towards the vaulted ceiling. The central dome was glass, tiny pieces cased in black diamond mullions. It cast light patterns on the floor below—

"Welcome, Lady Witch, to the Great Library of Corinna."

My muscles stiffened and I spun around. A woman stood before me, her gray robes the same color as her hair, pulled back into a tight chignon. Her features were timeless, slight and delicate. She was aging, but the fine lines did little to hide her beauty.

"I...thank you. This is..." I hardly had the words. The librarian gave a curt nod, as if this was the sort of reaction she gave to everyone that came here. "There must be thousands of books."

"Hundreds of thousands, Lady Witch. And many aren't on display." My lips formed into an '*oh*.' "You must be our new guest, here with Prince Aleksander? Yes, well then. Welcome. I am Nadia, high keeper. There are other keepers about, all of whom would be glad to help you in your search. Assuming you are here for something...specific?"

I hesitated. "Just...browsing. I am a great lover of books."

"As are we all."

"Do you have a section on the history of Corinna?"

"Of course. A popular section. You will find it in section D aisle forty-four."

"Perfect—wait. You said *keeper*? Is that—"

"The keepers of Corinna have kept the library since its beginning. We have weathered the years, stood the test of time, to protect and preserve our great collection. Here, you will find books from every country, those that still exist, and those that have fallen into mere memory. You will find books of knowledge, and books of pleasure, books of intrigue, and books of controversy. You will find that there is nothing, absolutely nothing, that isn't covered, in this great place."

She said these words as if she'd rehearsed them a thousand times. I studied her, my eyes attempting to peel back the layers. If she were a mere librarian, that would have been her title. I was tempted to push harder, but instead, I tucked it away. "Thank you."

She spared me a final, appraising look, then turned and calmly strode off, disappearing into an alcove.

"Keepers," I whispered to myself, grunting. "I bet there's a whole section on *that*, if this place is as extensive as she claims." I looked up again, taking in the levels that opened up and circled the atrium where I stood, intricate railings protecting patrons from falling to the mosaic tile beneath my feet. I counted—there were eight levels. I could have asked which one housed section D, but I was too eager to explore for myself.

I set off. Scattered throughout the stacks on the first level, scholars and patrons occupied sofas, tables, and alcoves. A deep hush filled the air, almost tangible. I couldn't help the smile spreading across my lips. No wonder Rixon loved books. No wonder he had so regularly occupied the library at the Citadel. Growing up with something like this at hand? He'd been lucky, in that respect.

I found what I was looking for on the second level; an entire section dedicated to the city of Corinna. History of kings, buildings, and even its founding. I zeroed in on that, pulling a stack of books before I located a table and set about reading.

Corinna was founded nearly two thousand years ago, making it one of the oldest settlements in Raeria. The land was discovered, *supposedly*, by explorers from Uscain, across the sea. According to my current text, the Uscanians had found a largely uninhabited stretch of wilderness and founded a shipping outpost, right here at the mouth of the river, which they later named *Runnel*. They hoped to make Corinna a gateway into the continent beyond. I read and read, trying to memorize things that felt more important.

Corinna is said to be the name of the ship that...

My eyes began to blur. I blinked, taking a deep breath. Forcing myself onward, I consumed paragraph after paragraph. Most of it was dry exposition. At times, I skimmed, searching for information about how the city was laid out, designed, engineered. My head jerked, nearly falling off my wrist. I blinked, focusing my gaze on the words. Too many sleepless nights were catching up with me.

How long had I been sitting here?

The scuff of a boot was my only warning. Two strong hands braced themselves on the table caging me in; Rixon's body pressed against my shoulders. "I should have known you'd find the library," he murmured, nipping at my ear. My insides curled as his scent washed over me, remnants of the soap we'd washed with, mixed with his characteristic musk. He laid a teasing kiss on my temple, then pulled up a chair beside me. He flipped it, sat down, and rested his forearms along the back.

"Well, hello." I looked him over. "How was the meeting?"

"Pure torture. You try sitting through hours of discussions on trade and tell me how you find it."

"Well, it can't be much better than this." I slid the open text his way.

He glanced down, grunting. "I could have told you where Corinna got its name, and how it came to be settled by the Uscainians." He reached out then, and rubbed his thumb over the corner of my mouth, failing to hide the twitch of his.

"Stop that!" I batted his hand away, ignoring his amusement at the drool that had apparently formed there.

"Well," he concluded, "I hope it wasn't a complete waste of time. Surely you found something?"

"You are so very lucky, Lord Wielder, that you are sitting there, and I am sitting here," I said, keeping my voice low. "It's been a challenge staying awake, and now you tell me I've only been learning details you already know? Fantastic. Utterly fantastic."

He chuckled. "I take it you're searching for some sort of information about the tunnels? We should inquire with the master builder."

"Firstly, I don't know who that is. Secondly, what makes you so sure this master builder of yours won't run straight to your father and tell him what we're up to?"

"So?" He lifted an eyebrow.

"*So*? The last thing I want is for him to know we're exploring the tunnels."

"Hm..." He rubbed the stubble along his jaw. "Suppose you've got a point."

I tried to fix him with a look, but his eyes were too unfocused to notice. Unlike me, he hadn't gotten the luxury of sleeping for another blessed hour. I captured my bottom lip between my teeth. "Are you free now?" I asked. "Or must you go back to work?"

He snorted, his eyes focusing on me again. "Free, I believe, but one never knows. I'm probably missing some sort of appointment with my betrothed to pick out napkins or some fucking ridiculous thing."

I burst into laughter, immediately clamping a hand over my mouth. Nearby, a scholar glanced up sharply, fixing me with a glare, before turning back to his books. "Well, as much as I enjoy being here, I could use some food."

"I was going to say the same," he drawled, but there was a hungry gleam to his eyes that had nothing to do with sustenance. Still, he said, "Why don't we shelve these and head out into the city?"

"I'd love nothing more."

The riverside cafe had a covered patio, with tables blanketed in white cloth, accented by little vases with a single flower. It was quaint and adorable, and I loved it immediately. I sat across from Rixon, the river to my left. Everywhere I glanced, there was something to look at. Mostly, it was at the passing vessels, all different styles, some with sails furled, others, flat barges heavy with cargo. They bore different flags, and Rixon surprised me by knowing them all, naming far off kingdoms I'd never heard of, each time I asked.

Most of the tables were full. The din of conversation was loud enough to keep ours hidden. Rixon spent a good deal of time telling me—in painful detail—about the council meeting, to punish me, mostly. But I pretended to listen throughout the meal, until he finally gave up and fell silent.

It wasn't as if *I* cared whether or not Lord Wallace had to pay import fees on wood. Or whether Lady Erwin needed to double the price of silk because one of her ships had been lost at sea. Rixon didn't seem to care, either. So, who could guess he'd find so many words—most of them riddled with colorful uses of *fuck*, and *fucking*, and *asshole*—to describe the whole thing. If it helped rid him of his frustration, I didn't mind.

I sighed, leaning back in my chair, trying to stretch my full belly. Gulls swooped near the river's edge, trying to snatch up whatever little bits they could find. It was a peaceful way to pass the middle of the day.

"So, you'd like to do a bit more digging in the library before we resort to more drastic measures?" Rixon asked.

"Hmm...?" I brought my mind back to the matter. "I think so, yes. There must be scrolls outlining the city, maps, that sort of thing. I could ask one of the keepers, perhaps one of the younger ones who will be less suspicious. I'm new to the city, after all. Why shouldn't I be curious to know my way around?"

"Because you have me to show you?"

"Oh, but you're *so busy* with all your new duties. You can't possibly be troubled."

"Right. Of course. How could I forget?" He lifted an eyebrow.

"What *are* the keepers, anyway?" I asked. "I mean, are they really just using a fancier name for librarian?"

"I believe they are something more than that. Scholars, in a sense. Historians. There are thousands of books to keep track of, to preserve, and care for. But I suppose...I've always just assumed they were fancy librarians, yes. I never questioned it."

"And now—?"

A server stepped over, clearing away our emptied plates, refiling our water glasses. Rixon waited, then said, "I do find it curious. But, who knows. Maybe they simply need to feel important."

I snorted. He lifted a shoulder, the corner of his mouth twitching. "I have another idea, too," I added.

"Oh?"

"When we go hunting tonight, I'd like to stay close to the docks."

"You're hoping a demon will come from the tunnels?" he asked. I bit my lower lip. "And if we must slay it?" he asked. "How do you propose we find our way out? We're stuck with the same conundrum. Getting lost under the city. Not all those tunnels had grates."

My eyes widened, the idea so simple we should have thought of it last night. "We can mark the walls, surely? That way we won't need a map."

"All right, then, no harm in giving it a try."

We paid for our meal and returned to the palace, stopping off at the stables on our way in. Jarrow and Ferrah were happy to see us. I promised them both some exercise, soon, when we settled in.

The afternoon rushed by in a blink. A nap, followed by a rough bout of sex, where Rixon fucked me on my knees, clinging to the corner bed post. And then the tailor's assistants were knocking on our door, delivering one of the gowns Marvin had completed after my initial fitting. I would never in a million years admit that I'd ruined the other.

Before I knew it, we were descending to the dining room, bracing ourselves for dinner with the king. It began far more smoothly than the last, for obvious reasons. I was just settling into my second course, when the king addressed me.

"I hear, Lady Witch, that you arrived in my city on the back of an Akeron."

I lifted my chin, hiding my surprise. "You heard correctly, Your Majesty." Those in our immediate vicinity paused their conversations to listen. I casually lifted my fork, taking another bite of my salad. Beside me, Rixon was tense.

"I didn't realize the Citadel had such a fine stock of horses to lend."

"They don't." At this, the king's brow arched. I wasn't sure why he was being conversational. A show, perhaps? Or maybe he was genuinely curious. But with so many ears, I didn't wish to stir things up. "Jarrow is mine. I brought him with me to the Citadel."

"Akerons are fine horses. Got a few myself," he added. "But when I heard the rumors, I was curious. So I decided to see for myself."

Beneath the table, my hand clenched. I hated the idea of him looking at my horse. Would he go so far as to harm him? No, probably not. Not unless he knew what Jarrow meant to me. And even then, it was unlikely. He was more likely to steal Jarrow than harm him.

"And?" I smoothed my voice, sounding merely curious.

"*And*, he is a fine horse. Finer than mine, even. How did you come by him?"

I blinked. There was nothing malicious in his voice. He genuinely wanted to know. I hid my surprise. I'd spent so long villainizing him, that it caught me off guard.

"My father fancies himself somewhat of a horse collector and expert," Rixon explained, failing to hide exactly what he thought of that.

"Mind your tongue, *boy*," the king said, turning back to me. I was careful to keep my face smooth. "Well?"

"I helped to birth him, if you must know. Akeron mares have a hard time of it, compared to most. Their narrow builds make it challenging. I had to drag him out."

The king's brows rose. "You know something of horses, then?"

Rixon snorted but said nothing.

"A fair bit more than you, I would wager," I answered, half expecting him to bristle at my obvious jibe.

Instead, he merely rubbed his chin. "You know what makes them prized, then? The Akeron?"

"Aside from their rarity? Akerons are a mixed breed, Your Majesty. Initially, they were regarded skeptically. A mix of Bravian to make them beautiful and smart, Lagara Quarter, to give them their speed, and Gypson Long for endurance. They are the only horse in their class. The only horse that can match a Gypson over long distance and get there in half the time. Perhaps not as showy as the Bravian, nor as good at short sprints, but still beautiful and fast."

"Not as fast as the Lagara, though. I'd wager my Lagaras against your Akeron in a short race."

"Would you?" Something inside me perked up.

The king lifted his goblet, eyeing me over the rim. "Got two that have never lost a race yet. Fastest in the kingdom."

I sat up straighter. "Where did you get them?"

"A rare breeder north-east of here, known for Lagaras and Akerons." A thrill raced over my skin. "Got quite a few from the man, some of my best."

"Anatol Krysinski?" I couldn't help myself.

The king scowled, in thought. "I do believe it was. Great breeder, that man. He used to visit the capital once a year, during the racing season, always brought prize winners along. I never passed up the chance to purchase a few."

My stomach swooped. Rixon turned to me. "Lady Witch? Are you all right?" I shook my head, clearing my thoughts, then nodded.

"You know him, then?" King Kozma asked, oblivious to the warring emotions in me. "I haven't seen the man in a decade or more. Never could be certain what happened to him."

"He died," I found myself saying. Flames tore across my vision. My ears echoed with the ring of their screams. I blinked, pushing the memories away.

The king frowned. "You..."

"He was my father," I said, hardly knowing what prompted the truth. I hoped he wouldn't use it against me.

He leaned back in his chair, falling silent. Perhaps what he saw in my expression kept the questions at bay. When he next spoke, he said, "I'd suspect you are correct then, that you know more about horses than I."

I balked. My chest swelled, lungs expanding. He shouldn't have made me feel this way. I wanted to hate him even more for it, and yet—

"What do you say we have a race?" The king sat forward again, eager.

This time, I frowned. Another game, then? But why?

"Are you trying to steal my horse?"

"It wouldn't be theft if I won him fairly."

I perked up. "A wager, then?"

A dangerous one, at that. I would never give Jarrow up. Never in a million years. And yet...

"All right. I do enjoy high stakes. I'd like to see how my fastest Lagaras measure up against the prized Akeron horse of Krysinski's stables."

I swallowed. "And Jarrow is your winning prize?"

"Yes. What is yours?"

My mind spun with possibility. We had an audience, those closest at the table. There were certain requests the king would outright refuse. My first thought was Trudy Holland—calling off the engagement. But that would have been worth little in the grand scheme of things. I planned to have Rixon far away from here before the wedding happened.

I needed something less selfish.

"The witches," I decided.

His expression turned wary. "What about them?"

"If I win, you allow the witches and their welders out after curfew to hunt demons in the streets."

He leaned back, something flashing across his expression. Then he smiled. I didn't exactly like the look of it. "Well, played, Lady Witch. Well played, indeed. All right. If my Lagaras win, I take Jarrow, if Jarrow wins, I shall fulfill your request."

Butterflies fluttered to life in my stomach. I didn't dare look at Rixon, even if I could picture his expression. His shock.

"What say you?" The king addressed the rest of the table. "A race, to offer up some entertainment?"

A feminine squeal—Trudy Holland clapped her hands together in delight. Others lifted their goblets indicating their agreement. There was no backing out now.

I sat up straighter in my chair. Something, nerves perhaps, prompted me to say, "Are you sure this is a good idea, Your Majesty? Jarrow is used to outrunning demons. A couple of Lagaras won't be so difficult."

My voice came out even, hiding my sudden misgivings.

Almost as if he could read my thoughts, he said, "There will be no backing out, now." He lifted his goblet and drank deeply. "Shall we say tomorrow afternoon, then? Two o'clock?"

I opened my mouth and spoke before I had the chance to reconsider. "You're on."

Chapter 16

Rixon

Rixon eyed his witch in the darkness. They stood outside the tunnel dumping into the river. "He's up to something." The words were out of his mouth before he could stop them.

"I'm not disagreeing," Mina said, biting her lip, peering into the darkness. "But I have my own agenda."

He trusted her. This was all part of her strategy. Winning the race would give her an upper hand in solving the demon issue.

He considered, then changed the subject. "Did you know?" His voice dropped low, serious.

"That my father sold the king horses? Yes, I had a hunch. He used to take the trip once a year. He would leave for about three weeks. He loved it, visiting the capital during the racing season. It's where he made his biggest fortunes. Selling to all the stables that brought competitors from all over Raeria."

Rixon grunted. He remembered those races as a boy, forced into attendance by his father. Despite his reluctance, once he was out of the palace, he enjoyed them. But he'd never felt the same love and eagerness that his father did.

"Jarrow will certainly be up for the task," he found himself saying. He didn't let himself consider the alternative—what would happen if Jarrow lost.

Mina laughed. He let the sweet sound of it brush over him, failing to hide the smile it brought. "He's a fierce competitor. He won't let anyone get the better of him."

"I would expect nothing less."

"I daresay he might even get violent, if it comes down to it. I would not be surprised if he sabotages the entire race, just to ensure he comes out in the lead."

Rixon looked over her expression. "You're actually excited about this, aren't you?"

"I...I shouldn't be. But, I'm a little nervous, too. I won't let him take Jarrow. I'll fight tooth and claw before that happens." Blackness bled into her eyes.

He stepped closer, lifting her chin with his index finger, kissing her lips. "My little witch, ever the competitor. Always has to be the best. Kill the most demons, study the hardest, learn the most magic. Well then, I am eager to see how you do."

She bit her lower lip and he had to step away to keep his hands off her. This wasn't the place to get distracted. They had work to do.

An hour passed, and then another. They paced before the opening, waiting. Not a single demon showed.

"You don't feel anything in the city?" Rixon found himself asking, patience wearing thin.

"Nothing beyond the strange pressure." She sighed, looking at the opening. "I'm going to go in," she decided. "If I have to wait here another moment, I'll go mad."

"Mina..." he warned.

"Give me one of your Nebrine knives." He hesitated, then pulled one from his baldric, handing it over. She walked through the bent bars of the tunnel's grate and stopped in the darkness. There, she proceeded to scratch the letter M into the wall. Nebrine was strong enough to cut through anything, including stone. He tried not to wince at the sound of a prized blade, cutting into the tunnel. When she pulled it back, the blade was unscathed. "There," she said, satisfied. "Now we just need some light."

He sighed, throwing her a warning glare. "Stay here."

He retrieved a torch from the nearest warehouse, then led Mina into the tunnels. At each junction, she scratched an M into the wall. M for *Mina*, most likely.

This time, he paid closer attention to their surroundings. Every once in a while, he found a square grate fixed along the tunnel ceiling. Little bits of light spilled in from each. Some dripped with muck of questionable contents, dumped into the streets. They dodged them, keeping closer to the wall to avoid being splashed.

Even still, he was soon coated in a layer of ick, eager for a bath. Most of the grates were small enough to fit a single body. Should they want to get up and out, he could remove one and hoist Mina through. He kept an eye out for larger ones, big enough to fit a demon. Eventually, the grates disappeared, replaced with a more solid roof as they moved deeper into the city, until there would be no getting out that way.

Their boots, even their pants, were soaked through. Not a single summoning star had been seen, or a demon, for that matter. They pressed on.

He might have been lost now, with no idea how to get back, were it not for the breadcrumbs Mina scattered. They were getting nowhere. He opened his mouth—

"Rixon, look!"

His mouth snapped closed. The walls had changed. "Stone," he said, lifting the torch, examining the nearest tunnel. "This one has nicer stone, while the others are a mix."

"Do you suppose it leads to the palace, then?"

"If I had to guess."

"Then let's go." They hastened their steps. The ground beneath his boots became solid. No mud, just a faint trickle of water. His boots still squelched as he walked, the soles water-logged. He thought of his room, of the warm bath waiting there—

Mina hissed.

"What is it?" he said, rounding on her. The torch threw her features into stark relief.

"Demons," she said, head darting back and forth.

"Here?" His heart kicked up.

"I...I don't know." She frowned.

His ears pricked. "There, do you hear that?"

Somewhere in the distance, the faint roar of something familiar. A Jarg, perhaps?

"Follow me," Mina said, turning on her heel, away from the direction they'd been heading. They took off at a sprint. Mina cut right, a different direction than they'd come, not bothering to follow the marks. Then she cut left, and right again—

He crashed into her back, snaking an arm about her waist to keep them upright. "We need to go up," Mina said, breathless.

"You mean—"

"I don't know. I don't know where it came from, but it's not in the tunnels."

He swore, glancing about. "This way." They took off again, leaving the nicer tunnels behind, making their way back into the city.

"There! I see light." She dragged him to the nearest overhead grate. Another bellow had them scurrying. Mina lifted her hand. With magic, the grate above them was ripped away, flung outward on its hinges.

Well, that was easy.

Mina turned to him, eyes dancing, blackening. She slipped his dagger into his baldric. He dropped and laced his fingers together. "I'll hoist you." She didn't hesitate, slipping a mucky booted foot into his hands. He grimaced at the filth of it, lifting. She scrambled up and out. He followed after, jumping to get his hands in place, then hauling himself through the opening.

They emerged, two filthy sewer rats, into chaos. Guards shouted, circling around a cluster of demons. He spotted the Jarg he'd heard bellowing, and two Trongs. Mina had led them exactly where they needed to be. Once again, her abilities unnerved him.

He took in the scene before him. "Fucking hell," he muttered. With swords out, the six guards were taking swipes at the demons. A few stood farther back, afraid to get close.

"Step back," Mina commanded. She'd drawn a hood over her face to hide the change in her eyes. Several heads swung their way. He strode forward, pulling his sword free, then took off in a run. He had the first head rolling with a single swipe. It cost him, though. Pain erupted through his sword arm. With his free hand, he snatched a Nebrine blade from his baldric and swiped down, removing the pincer that had clamped on tight. The Trong hissed, but he was already spinning, dodging forward, driving forward with his sword. He thrust upward, right through its skull. Another swipe of his knife removed another pincer. He ripped his sword free, removed the first Trong's head, then spun to fully face the second. He backed away a step, catching his breath, removing the detached pincer from his arm, wincing as it came free. Dodging another swipe, he removed the final Trong's support legs, then swung up and around, letting its head follow seconds later.

Silence fell.

Mina stood by, watching. She hadn't immobilized any of them, he realized. When he saw the shocked expressions on the guards' faces, he believed he knew why.

"That was..." one of them said, trailing off.

"I've never seen anything like that, Your Highness," another said. The rest of them gathered their senses and bowed. He was surprised they had even recognized him, covered in muck as he was.

"Go for their heads, next time," he advised, holding his sword forward for Mina. She knew what to do without his asking—using her fire magic to incinerate the ick on the blade so he could sheathe it.

She disposed of what was left, until there was no sign the demons had been there.

"They didn't come from the tunnels," he mused, guiding her away.

"We don't know that for certain."

"Wouldn't we have heard them?"

"That network is extensive, Rixon. They could have passed by us using a different tunnel. There are many of them, and the grates are easy enough to remove." She appeared thoughtful. "Let's drop by the inn. I want to see if anything is amiss."

They did exactly that, circling the *King's Mantle*, looking for strange clues. Eventually, they made their way up to the roof across the street, to keep watch. No one came or went. That didn't mean anything. The witch who summoned tonight's demons could have returned before they'd finished slaying them. Assuming it had been a witch, but what else could draw a demon from the depths of hell?

Eventually, they abandoned their watch.

The sky was brightening when they made their way back to the palace. The gate guards hardly recognized them. Once again, they stripped their clothes in the doorway of his chambers, careful to keep from tracking muck through his apartments. Moving in unison, without a single word, they both gravitated towards the bath.

He let out a pleased groan, sinking into the hot water. Mina set about healing his wound, tisking over the injury, her brow furrowed as she knit the skin back together. They washed each other, the motions so familiar, it was second nature. With uncontrolled yawns, they tumbled into bed before the sun even crested the palace walls. He wrapped himself around the woman he loved, nuzzling his nose into her neck, shoving a knee between her thighs, and dropped into sleep before he could even wish her a good night.

Mina thrashed against him, breathing hard. He sat up, pulling her into his arms. Light spilled into the room through the drapes, but no one had been by to pull him from his slumber. "Another nightmare?" He rested his lips against her temple, felt her nod, felt her muscles loosen. "The same thing?" he asked. She nodded again.

She'd been dreaming of the rift. Frequently. Of the things she'd seen when they'd closed it.

He held her body against his, letting her calm before considering the best way to make love to her. She settled in against him. Perhaps he'd let her ride him, this time—

"Oh, gods!" She shot out of his arms and off the bed. He frowned. "It's nearly lunch! The race! I need to get to the stables."

He rolled his eyes, flopping onto his back, propping an elbow under his head. "Lady Witch, you have time aplenty. Come and ride my cock before you scamper off for your race."

"No." A look of defiance crossed her expression.

"No?" He lifted onto his elbows. "Did you just tell me *no*? Here? In the bedroom? If you don't get that tight cunt over here and settle on my cock in the next five seconds, I'm going to spank you so hard, you won't be able to sit in Jarrow's saddle. You can kiss your race goodbye, then."

A red tinge crept up her neck. Meanwhile, her eyes blackened. She regarded him, glancing towards the wardrobe and then his cock, tenting the sheets. She pulled her lower lip between her teeth.

"One..." he counted. She sighed, shoulders falling. "Two. Three. Four—"

"All right, all right!" She walked over, ripping the sheet back and climbing atop his naked body, straddling his hips without lowering herself. "You are *insufferable*." Her tender expression mitigated her words. She leaned forward and kissed him, gently, then reached for his cock. With one hand pressed against his chest, the other rubbing the head between her slit, she began to ease him inside of her.

He growled. Sensation erupted, racing up the length of his shaft, burying deep in his center. That brought a mischievous grin to her lips. He shivered as he watched her work, as she buried him to the hilt.

Mina rode him the same way she rode her horse, with all the experience and agility, all the grace and wild abandon he'd come to love. "You are exquisite," he said between gasps, unable to keep his hands from her hips, unable to keep himself from thrusting up into her. They climaxed together, breathing hard, eyes wide as they watched each other. His heart flapped, watching her wring every last drop of himself free inside her. Then, she collapsed on his chest.

It had lasted mere minutes, but those minutes felt like a lifetime. She shifted slightly, and his cock gave a torturous spasm, still rocked by the aftershocks of his orgasm. His fingers stroked the smooth skin of her back.

"Good girl," he purred, pleased. She nuzzled closer, rubbing her nose against him before kissing his skin. "You're going to win today," he said. "I want to see the look on my father's face when he loses to you. Do whatever it takes."

She snorted, peeling herself up enough to look at him. "I was already planning on it. But thanks." She tilted her head. "Don't you have a council meeting or some other matter you're missing?"

He shrugged, his movements lazy. "Wouldn't know—don't remember. My father's going to have to get me my own personal assistant if he hopes I'll keep my responsibilities sorted."

She huffed. He watched her, sitting up now, still wrapped about him with her wet heat. The light made her pale skin glow. Her black hair was a mess of tangles, falling nearly to her waist. She'd let it get longer since they'd first paired.

His heart squeezed. He was struck then, as he often was, by her beauty, her grace. By what he felt for her. Love didn't do it justice. They were tied together by so much more than that. By more than their bond. It was as if their very souls were entrenched within the confines of each other, rooted, tangled, the way her two magics were.

"What's that look for?" she said, studying him.

He made a sound in the back of his throat.

"Oh, come on. Tell me."

He hesitated and then, "You mean more to me than anything in the world. There is nothing I wouldn't do for you, to keep you safe, to keep you for myself."

Her eyes darkened. She bit her lip, studying him. Then her hips gently rocked and he was aching again, desperate to move inside her. In one smooth motion, he flipped their positions and made love to her as he'd done the day before—a record, perhaps. But he needed to show her exactly what his words meant.

"Riders, in position!" came the cry that had everyone's attention snapping upright. Rixon's heart kicked up, pounding against his chest. The arena was nearly empty, save for those in the king's circle, permitted to take part.

"Shall we take bets?" Trudy asked him. He shot his father a glare. Trudy clasped her hands in glee. "I do so *love* a good wager."

"Then, by all means," he drawled, "don't let me stop you."

Her face flushed. She turned her attention back to the matter at hand, his dismissal clear. A pinch of guilt needled his skin. It wasn't *her* fault she'd been roped into this, but he certainly took it out on her when he could. He inhaled, letting his breath out slowly.

Earlier, he'd walked with Mina through the city, leading Jarrow by the reins. She'd donned a pair of cropped riding breeches tucked into tall boots, and a sleek white tunic that fitted her curves perfectly. Her hair was tied back, the long black tail cascading down her back. The sight of it earlier had his fingers itching. He'd exercised control to keep from wrapping it around his fist. So many dirty thoughts in his mind...

His eyes remained fixed on her, even now. She was mounted in her saddle, Jarrow perfectly motionless beneath her. She'd spent the entire walk whispering things to him. "He's never done a race like this before," she had explained, when they'd gotten him situated behind the gate. And yet, Jarrow seemed to know exactly what was happening. He didn't show a single measure of discomfort, getting closed inside the bars with her.

Rixon's chest swelled. She'd win. On a horse that wasn't bred for this, with a rider that had never partaken in an official race. It would be impressive. He intended to show her exactly how much, later.

"Riders, at the ready!" the announcer called. He tensed, on the edge of his seat. Everyone seemed to tip forward, leaning in towards the track—

The gong sounded. The gates were thrown wide. Three finely bred horses shot onto the track.

He surged to his feet, heart in his throat. The small crowd burst into screams of delight. Before he realized it, Jarrow's name was on his lips, shouted at the top of his lungs.

CHAPTER 17

MINA

I knew how to ride. I'd seen my father train jockeys at our ranch. I'd even participated a time or two, for fun. But nothing, *nothing*, prepared me for the exhilaration that came as the gates burst open and Jarrow shot free.

My pulse pounded in my ears, mingling with the screams from the risers. Faintly, I thought I heard Rixon, too, shouting for Jarrow. My body flooded with warmth. I couldn't imagine what it would be like on a real race day, the stadium packed, thousands of voices screaming. It was infectious, those voices, my adrenaline, the sound of pounding hooves as we broke free.

I lifted in my saddle, adopting the sleek positioning of the other jockeys beside me. My body remained loose and fluid, absorbing the movements as Jarrow swallowed up the ground beneath him. *"Makka! Makka, Jarrow!"* I cried, urging him on. *Faster*!

His ears pricked. He knew.

Beside me, two beautiful Lagaras kept pace. They were both lightly colored, with beige coats and silky, cream colored manes. Their tails were kept long and untouched. I'd opted to braid Jarrow's and tuck it up, for show, mostly. I'd also given him little braids along his sleek, black mane.

Lagaras were bred for this. The king's were prized, having already established a well known track record. Beside me, the jockeys shouted encouragement, their voices mingling with the Aavix I used to urge Jarrow onward.

The track was oval, soft dirt. It flung up behind us in our wake. I calculated the distance. We needed to make it around the ring of the track, two straights and two curves, and be the first to finish. *"Makka, Jarrow!"* I cried again.

Jarrow snorted, then swung his head sideways and nipped his teeth, attempting to frighten the beige stallion on our right. I didn't bother scolding him. The stallion, *Petzi*, only snorted, pushing harder to inch ahead. On *Petzi's* right, *Kalli* gained half a head over us. I groaned, urging Jarrow ahead.

We passed the small crowd in the stands, their shouts mingling with pounding hooves. A brief glimpse showed Rixon on his feet, hands braced on the barrier, leaning forward. We approached the first curve of the oval track. Both Lagaras began pulling ahead.

My heart surged, adrenaline pumping. I needed to win this. For Jarrow, for the witches, to free them of the curfew.

Petzi and *Kalli*. They were names my father had chosen, I was certain of it. In Aavix, *Petzi* meant *wind* and *Kalli* meant *fire*. Wind and fire. Fitting names—names my father would have selected with care. Names to represent their personalities.

Emotion slammed into my chest, shocking and unbidden. My eyes blurred. I blinked, attempting to clear them. What would he think of me, if he saw me racing the king's horses? Horses he'd bred to win at all costs? A tear came free at the corner of my eye, streaking along my temple. I missed him so much it hurt.

My stomach sank.

Suddenly I hated the thought of winning—beating my father's Lagaras. It was like spitting on his efforts, his life's work. A small part of me wilted, the heat of shame prickling my cheeks; I never should have accepted this race. Rounding the corner of the track, both Lagaras pulled forward by a head's length—

A flutter of wings made my breath catch. A dark chuckle seeped into my thoughts.

"With blood we shed, with blood we keep..."

The hairs on the back of my neck prickled. The feeling of being watched grated down my spine. Jarrow's ears pricked, as if he could sense it, too. But Jarrow was used to demons in close proximity. Used to outrunning them.

A horse's scream split the air. A head's length ahead of us, *Petzi's* eyes rounded, the whites showing. Beside him, *Kalli* reacted similarly. Shouts, as their jockeys attempted to calm them. It was no use. They faltered, tossing their heads, thwarting their gain.

My eyes darted around, searching for the source. The winged demon was here—it had to be. The pull in my chest was undeniable. But...it was nowhere in sight.

The Lagaras began to fall back.

The small crowd gave echos of surprise. Both horses continued protesting, still sprinting, but distracted. The final straight shrank, the curve coming upon us. Jarrow began pulling ahead; I didn't know whether to slow him or spur him on. Taking this sudden advantage felt like cheating. But Jarrow was used to one thing, and one thing only: outrunning demons.

Another flutter of wings made my stomach dip.

I discerned the moment Jarrow's instinct kicked in. We rounded the bend, pulling nearly a full length ahead of *Petzi*. The finish line was there—a few breaths more. The dark laughter echoed in my mind. "Stop doing that," I hissed, overcome with fury. It didn't matter.

We crossed the finish line, *Petzi* and *Kalli* on our heels, their heads still pivoting in fear. Right as Jarrow plunged across the line, Petzi's head slammed into his flank. Jarrow squealed, nimbly dancing away. His foot twisted, sank into the sand, and he stumbled before pulling himself upright. I cursed, jumping from his back.

A hush fell over the crowd. I didn't pay it any attention. All three horses had come to a stop. *Petzi* and *Kalli* were still stamping, eyes wild. Several attendants rushed over. I spotted the king among them, Rixon, too.

I felt the demon's presence recede, then disappear entirely. My anger remained, hot and piercing. Jarrow looked calm as ever, but I saw the pain in his eyes. He took a limping step forward, then stopped. He held his front leg slightly off the ground, keeping it free of his weight.

I swore under my breath, glancing at the other two horses. I knew what had happened. In his fright, *Petzi's* swinging head had come too close to jarrow, had struck him accidentally. Jarrow didn't take kindly to other horses in his personal space. He had gotten surprised. He'd misstepped.

"What happened?" the king roared, coming to a stop beside us. "Did you use your magic to rig the race?!" he demanded.

What?!

"How *dare*—no, Your Majesty. I would never do such a dirty thing." Something in my chest thumped. "The horses are frightened. They reacted."

"Yes, and I would like to know *why*. You used your magic to frighten them. Our bet is forfeit. I will not grant you your request."

My muscles pulled tight. "I am the daughter of a horse breeder. I would never stoop to such measures. I would never tamper with a horse's emotions. I wouldn't even know how."

"Father—"

"Never mind that *your* Lagara collided with mine and caused an ankle sprain," I continued, ignoring the fact that Rixon tried to intervene.

The king took several deep, calming breaths, assessing the situation. Earlier, he'd been in a good mood. I'd almost allowed myself to think this would end well. And perhaps it might have, had that fucking demon not shown itself.

"I want a rematch," the king insisted, but his voice was no longer jovial as it had been earlier. It was brittle and accusing.

"Jarrow's ankle is sprained. I'm not letting him do a single thing until I heal it."

"I think that's enough for one day," Rixon said, voice firm.

The king continued to regard me, suspicion in his eyes. Before, there'd been only excitement. My nostrils flared. I didn't deserve his accusations. I wasn't going to sit here and pleadingly defend myself against something I hadn't done. But fine. He wanted to make *me* the villain? Fine.

"My horses were in the lead," the king said, as if it needed to be known.

I pulled my shoulders back. "Yes? And? They lost. Need I remind you, Your Majesty, this race was your idea, not mine." And already, I regretted agreeing to it.

The king regarded me, expression cold. "See to your horse, Lady Witch." He turned on his heel and strode from the arena, his attendants rushing after him. He'd lost this round—whatever game he was playing. I couldn't help but think he didn't intend to lose the next. Whatever that might be, I needed to tread extra carefully henceforth.

Moments later, the other two horses departed. I simply stood there, watching everyone go their separate ways. Rixon planted himself before me, hands on his hips, eying me.

"What happened?"

"A demon." That was all I gave him—hardly an explanation. I clenched my jaw, trying to settle my anger. Jarrow's head nudged me. I turned to him. "*Shi kek, lekke roy,*" I said. *I know, pretty boy.*

I knelt down, assessing his leg, his ankle. He tensed, muscles going taut when I moved it, but at least it wasn't broken. I closed my eyes, pulling from my magic, and set about healing him. I'd healed flesh injuries for Jarrow, but never something like this. I wasn't as familiar with horse anatomy as I was with human anatomy, but my knowledge of horses in general helped. I worked on the inflammation and mended the torn tissue.

"They're now," I said. "Try that." I released his leg. Jarrow placed his foot gently at first, then leaned his full weight on it. "How's that?" I asked, standing up. He took a few tentative steps forward, neighed, then began prancing in a circle.

My foul mood evaporated. A barked laugh fell from my lips. "Yes, all better, hmm?" Jarrow tossed his head. "You were perfect, you know."

My horse preened.

Even as I said those words, a certain truth settled upon me. The Legaras had pulled ahead, right before the demon had appeared. "He would have won," I admitted, turning to Rixon. "Your father, the Lagaras. They were bred for this. I almost wanted them to—because of my father."

Jarrow was never meant to be a quarter horse, even if he was special.

"They are your father's legacy," Rixon said, his voice low. He took my face in his hands, running his thumbs over my cheeks. His own was full of understanding. "Now, do you want to talk about why they *didn't*?"

"That stupid, *fucking* demon," I hissed, mood darkening.

"So it's here then? In the city?"

I took a deep, steadying breath, then nodded and said, "Come, let's get Jarrow settled first. Then I'll tell you."

Rixon eyed me, like he was going to argue. Finally, he motioned me forward with his head. We were silent for a time, making our way from the arena, walking Jarrow through the city, back to the royal stables.

"It's here in the city. I'm pretty certain of it. It's been saying things to me. Strange things, about blood and sacrifice, and darkness. None of it makes any sense. And laughter—always this smug, chilly laugher."

Rixon hid his surprise, but I noticed the way his body tensed, the way his jaw tightened. "This has been going on since we arrived?"

"A couple of days, yes," I admitted, needled with guilt that I hadn't told him sooner. "It's why I looked so distraught the other day."

He gave a curt nod, running a hand over his hair, which was pulled back into a warrior knot today. Ready to get it off my chest, I told him everything. The fluttering wings, the way the demon was always just outside of my periphery, and the way it made my skin crawl.

Rixon's expression darkened with each word. "You should have told me."

My stomach dropped at his reprimand. It was rare for him to do it, which meant my actions had thoroughly angered him. I hated the thought of him angry with me.

While there were times we kept things from each other, this was something that concerned us both. Demons were common ground. He had every right to know, especially because it concerned my safety.

"I'm sorry," I managed, making sure to hold his gaze as I said it. Making sure he understood that I was.

He hesitated, then nodded. "You'll tell me if you hear it again? If you see it?"

"I will."

We entered through the palace gate. I ignored the brief but minor flare of discomfort that came with doing so. It had gotten worse, and I suspected why. It was the same reason I could do nothing to open them the other night.

We got Jarrow settled. Kam appeared, Aleck in tow, carrying a small sack of apples and a wreath of flowers. "Figured he'd be hungry after a race like that," Aleck said. Both he and Kam had come along, to look after the king's Lagaras. "Here you go, boy. You *did* win, after all."

I reached out to stop Aleck, then hesitated. A laugh burst from my lips as Jarrow leaned his head down, allowing the wreath to be placed around his neck. "Normally, he'd try and bite your fingers off. But I think he'd rather wear the wreath."

"He's a vain fellow—aren't you, Jarrow?" Kam said.

Rixon merely shook his head and went to lean against the stable wall, arms crossed, watching us. I took several apples from the sack and fed them to the victor. "You did a splendid job," I told him in Aavix, offering more praise beyond what I'd said at the track. "You're the bestest boy, aren't you?" Jarrow merely snorted and peeled his lips back from his giant, blocky teeth, then snickered, searching for another apple.

It was nearly dinnertime by the time we left, heading back to Rixon's rooms. My feet dragged along the corridor walkway. "The king's going to be pleasant tonight, I'm sure."

"We could always dine at the inn," Rixon ventured. "Either way, if we decide to go hunting, we'll be stuck outside until dawn."

I perked up. "There've got to be other ways into the palace," I mused, hating that we were stuck outside until dawn each night. "Even the Citadel had catacombs running beneath, with passages leading into the city."

"I'm sure there are." he drawled. "But we'd have to find them first, before we can use them."

I turned to him, grinning. "I vote for dinner at the inn and tunnels after that."

"Very well, Lady Witch." We entered his chambers, and I made for the bathing chamber to prepare for a long night.

We'd been so close to a discovery last night, before we'd been interrupted. So close to finding something in those tunnels. All our marks remained, we could follow them, save time, and head straight to the ones that ran under the palace.

Goosebumps spread over my skin as I shed my clothes. I couldn't help but feel we were on the verge of something. Like a word at the tip of my tongue, just out of reach. But that also meant something more. What would we face once we *did* get beneath the palace, and would it bring the answers I so desperately needed to find?

There was only one way to be certain.

CHAPTER 18

RIXON

Rixon began to relax, the muscles in his shoulders easing as he sipped his wine. Conversation buzzed around him, filling the inn's dining room with a comfortable level of background noise. The present company had grown on him, just a little. He didn't talk, but he enjoyed listening to Mina chatter away with the other witches. She sat between Anne and Elianna, both of whom she'd grown closer to since their arrival. He'd been forced to sit across from her, between their two wielders.

"And how deeply have you explored the city so far?" he found Mina asking, as she attempted to draw Lola into a conversation.

"Very little, just the areas surrounding the inn," Lola quietly said.

"She doesn't get out much," Anne offered up, rolling her eyes.

"Oh, let her be," Elianna scolded. "Not everyone is a chatty busybody eager to immerse themselves in the public eye."

He watched Mina take note of this—saw her mind working. She'd been at it all evening, asking loaded questions that might offer clues. They both wanted to know, were the witches behind the demon increase?

When dinner ended, Mina covertly pulled Anne and Elianna aside, leading them out onto the front porch. In a hushed voice, she told them about her suspicions. Rixon watched silently, knowing all too well that she'd isolated them on purpose. Perhaps to see their reaction, or perhaps because she trusted them enough to be truthful.

"You...you think a witch could be behind this?" Anne hissed, trying to whisper. "That...that—"

"It would explain why there are demons in the city," Elianna finished for her. "It's a valid consideration, actually. I thought about it myself, a time or two."

"But, why ask us? It could very well be me." Anne lifted her brows before adding, "Wait, do you think it is me? Is that why you've pulled us out here?"

"Anne, will you let the woman talk? Gods! What have we discussed about listening, *hmm*?"

"That listening is for people who haven't got things to say."

"That is *not*—"

"Yes, yes, I know," Anne groused.

Mina watched the two bicker, a smile pulling at her lips. "Well then," Mina said when they'd calmed down. "I don't have any solid proof. I've considered the possibilities. It seems the most plausible. Unless there's a rift hiding somewhere, but that seems less likely because we've searched and found nothing. A rift is a permanent scourge on the land, a star can be moved, recast."

He rubbed at his chin, fingers scraping against the growing stubble, as he watched Mina work.

"Summoning stars would allow someone to pull demons within the city's walls." Elianna mused. "But...how would the demons get free of the stars, after they're summoned?"

"Stars can be broken—from the outside." Both witches narrowed their eyes, looking at Mina. "I only know as of recently, and only because an ex-council witch gave me a lesson."

Elianna crossed her arms. "Is that so?"

Mina lifted her chin but didn't defend herself.

Anne said, "So...if it's happening, one of *our* witches could be summoning them? Breaking the circles, letting them out into the city?"

Elianna snorted, even though a knowing gleam lit her brown eyes. "You didn't pull us out here to accuse us, did you?" Mina shook her head. "I should have known. You want us to do a little sleuthing?"

They'd watched the inn without finding anything. Mina's tactics were changing. She wanted someone on the inside.

"If it wouldn't be too much trouble? If one of our witches is doing it, I doubt they're doing it here, out in plain sight. But you know them better than I do."

"They'd find somewhere else unnoticed," Elianna concluded. Mina nodded.

"So we keep an eye on comings and goings? And follow them when we can?" Anne piped up. "I like it. True detective work. I'm in."

Elianna sighed, eying Anne fondly. "As if *that's* a surprise."

"Oh, come on, Eli! We've been *so* bored. This could be fun."

"Be careful," Mina cautioned. "This could be very dangerous. If it is a witch and you're caught..."

"We will be careful," Elianna confirmed.

"Good. Well, then. Take care of yourselves." Mina hesitated, then stepped forward, giving them hugs. Rixon hid his surprise at her show of affection.

"You be careful as well," Elianna said, before nodding at Rixon. "Take care of her."

"I always do," he replied, his voice low and full of meaning.

It took over an hour to navigate their way back through the tunnels. They found the stone passage using the marks Mina had made. Rixon took the lead, holding his torch aloft.

The first set of bars were locked. Mina took a hairpin from her chignon, then glanced at him. "What?"

"Nothing, Lady Witch." The corner of his mouth twitched.

"No, really. What is that look for? You expect me to break it open with my magic? You *do* realize that would blow the gate off its hinges. It would cause quite a ruckus."

"I never said that."

"Okay...?"

When she still stared accusingly, he sighed and said, "Was merely wondering what made you so confident at picking locks."

"Oh." She hesitated, the hairpin hovering. "Well, I'll have you know that there were many books in the Citadel's library that were off limits to witchlings."

"You broke into the restricted section?" He blurted. She arched her brow. "Unbelievable. How very naughty, Lady Witch." Even in the torchlight, he spotted the telltale pink flush creeping up her neck.

"If you must know," she tutted, "I had a curious mind and didn't like the librarians asking questions."

"Well, then. Let's see your work."

She tsked, but set to work on the old gate. It didn't take long. Locks like these were merely a deterrent, so he wasn't all that surprised. But he did appreciate the look of Mina's pride as she finished.

He stared at her, chest swelling with warmth, until she caught his eye and offered a shy grin.

Beneath the palace, they found a passage that led to the dungeons, then doubled back. Another led to a massive storage room, packed with mountains of old furniture, long forgotten.

Mina picked through it for a few minutes, entertained, before they moved on. A number of passages had stairways leading upwards, places within the palace walls.

They left those for later.

Mina used one of his Nebrine blades to scratch tiny Ms into the stonework. These she made much smaller, so they'd go unnoticed. Hours passed in curious exploration.

When they found a locked gate that took them directly into the library's basement stacks, he'd have thought they found buried treasure. "So *this* is where they keep all the hidden ones," Mina breathed. "There are so many!" She clapped her hands together before placing them against her chest, over her heart, blinking with glee. "Let's explore," she decided, racing off into the dim light. Here, wall sconces were lit. This area was meant to be occupied more frequently than the rest of the places beneath the palace. But only by the keepers of the library.

"Be careful," he cautioned, in case anyone lurked. He didn't want word reaching his father.

Mina crept about, darting down row after row of books bound in aging hides, so worn he could hardly read the titles. He stayed close on her heels, torch aloft. Some sections contained floor to ceiling scrolls, rolled tight, piled atop each other. It was a place lost in time, crumbling with decay.

At the far end, Mina came to a stop. His muscles tensed. "What's the matter?" he whispered, his lips close to her ear.

"It's...there's..." She pressed a hand against her chest—a motion he'd grown accustomed to.

"Demons?"

"No...no." She shook her head, side to side, a repetitive motion, staring forward. "Something else."

He followed her gaze, saw the stone wall before her, then frowned. "Well, well, well..."

The space before them was incongruent, the stones a different color. *Nebrine*. And beside the pattern of Nebrine he found a worn catch. Without thinking, he pressed it. Grating rock made him flinch. The entire section of Nebrine swung inward. He glanced over his shoulder, eyes surveying the deserted stacks behind them.

Mina sucked in a breath, then darted inside before he could stop her. He followed, close on her heels, swinging the wall shut behind them. They'd found another corridor, this one much wider and better lit.

Mina took off at a quick pace, as if drawn towards something. "I can feel it, Rixon," she whispered, glancing toward him with darkening eyes, glazing over. "It's *calling* me."

He faltered. The hairs on the back of his neck rose. He reached for her—

She slipped from his grasp and turned right, down another tunnel. This one looked ancient. At the end, she made a left, then she stopped, gasping. He bumped against her, his hands reaching to grasp her shoulders.

He looked up. "What the fuck?!"

It was an octagonal room nearly twenty feet in diameter, wall sconces flickering, casting long shadows. But that was, perhaps, the least impressive aspect. His lips parted, eyes darting. He didn't know where to look first. The floor was made of an intricate mosaic stonework, all blacks and grays, with an inlaid five pointed star. He did a double take, then frowned. The walls were a burst of color, as if painted yesterday.

"Demons," he rasped, searching for his voice.

"What...what *is* all this?" Mina managed. She took a step forward but he tightened his hold. "No," she said, pulling free. "I want to see it, Rix."

He gave a curt nod, though she couldn't see that he had.

Something in him itched as she stepped into the room, walking to its center, turning in a circle. After a deep breath, he did the same. From floor to ceiling, murals had been painted, telling a story. It took him several moments to figure out what. Battles. They were *battles*. Legions of human armies, swords raised, shields braced, facing off against hordes of demons. He blinked. Piles of bodies littered the battlefield. At the forefront of the depiction, a man rode on horseback—no, a king, wearing...his father's crown.

His throat went dry.

He stood there, picking through each one. Minutes passed, or perhaps hours. Each detail was painted as if...as if the artist had been right there amidst the chaos, witnessing every moment. As if something like this had really happened long, long ago.

"What *is* this place?" Mina repeated, voice wavering. He couldn't answer—couldn't find the words. She spun towards the farthest wall, opposite the entry, then gravitated towards it. This was the only wall void of art, save for the elegant archway painted into the stone. It had scrolling letters along the arch, words, a poem. Except—

"I've never seen anything *like* this." Mina reached out.

He darted forward, wrapping his fingers around her wrist. "Don't—touch it, Lady Witch," he hissed, eying the arch. It looked so very like a doorway, were it not made of solid stone. He blinked, then frowned. The stone flickered and his stomach soured.

There were streaks across the center, some of them aged, others fresh, all the color of—

"Blood!" Mina gasped, stepping closer, but keeping her hands to herself. His palm itched. He reached for it, rubbing his thumb across the childhood scar, unconsciously. "Why is there blood smeared on it?"

Chills skittered down his arms, setting the hairs on end. "We should leave," he bit out. He didn't know why, except that he wanted to be far, far away from here. Something in his memory flashed, but it slipped away before he could grab it. A...familiarity.

"Look," Mina said. "Sometimes it flickers, like the stone is turning to liquid. It's...it's *calling* to me, Rix. It *wants* me."

"Mina, we need to leave," he said again, more forcefully. "Now." He grabbed her hand. She hesitated, brow furrowed. Then she rubbed at her chest, eyes going unfocused, allowing him to lead her out of the room.

He practically dragged her, desperate to put distance between them. With each step, a weight was lifted. He took a deep inhale. Mina appeared to relax, too. Her glazed, blackened eyes sharpened, returning to normal. They didn't speak. Not when they retreated through the ancient stacks, not when they made their way through the passages, not even as they emerged back into the dirt tunnels under the city.

Their desire to find a secret way into the palace was all but forgotten. Trumped by this new, frightening thing they'd found. And yet, neither of them spoke a single word.

Chapter 19

Mina

Some things are too frightening to be voiced. We didn't speak of the strange room we'd found under the palace. Not after dawn broke across the sky, and we were permitted entry to the palace. Not when we bathed and tumbled into bed, exhausted. Not even as Rixon prepared for another odious council meeting later that morning, announced when his father's assistant banged on our door to wake him.

We didn't speak of it at lunch, nor that afternoon, when we visited the library so Rixon might collect more reading material, nor when we took Jarrow and Ferrah out for a ride beyond the city walls. We certainly didn't speak of it when we visited Cora.

No, we didn't speak of it at all.

But that didn't mean it wasn't thought of. It had been on my mind, consuming me since the moment I'd felt it, since the moment I stepped foot into that awful room. The oppressive weight I'd felt since entering the city, was finally unearthed. It reminded me of a rift, and yet, not quite.

Each time I opened my mouth to voice my suspicions, I closed it almost immediately. Rixon had been distant. The sight had scared him more than he cared to admit. I allowed him this kindness, so that he might come to terms with his fear.

But it was more than that.

In hiding from what we'd found, I could also hide from what I'd felt. The pull to walk right through the arch had been undeniable, even if it had looked like nothing more than a wall. The idea was absurd—that I might walk right through.

When I finally suggested that we venture back down there, Rixon flat out refused. I would have forced the matter, except for the expression on his face. The same expression he wore the day we'd come across a horde of demons during our travels. The way he'd looked at me in those final moments before battle —I'd hoped to never see it again.

So we didn't venture down into the tunnels. When another day came and passed, we avoided it again. Soon, an entire handful of days came and went, and I was no closer to solving the mystery.

That's not to say I languished.

I spent hours in the library, looking for anything that might help me understand what I'd seen. I spent countless hours wandering the palace, deep in my mind, thinking about the murals. But, it was the archway, the words branded into my mind, that I couldn't forget.

I had recognized them, heard them before. So at last, when we'd been here for a little over a week, I ventured to the *one place* I might get answers. I took my sketch book and got comfortable, sitting on the parapet, overlooking the city below. I had already recreated several murals, crudely, from memory. I'd also drawn the arch, but I couldn't quite remember all the words, so I left that empty. As I sketched, I waited.

And then...I heard it. The flutter of wings, a flash in my peripheral. I stayed still as its dark chuckle sounded in my mind. I kept my book open, the pages splayed and visible. The presence grew closer, until I felt it like a threatening cloud at my back.

"So...you have seen Uzzamon. The gateway into our world."

Chills spread over my skin, even in the daylight. I didn't dare move, didn't dare scare it off.

"I have seen it," I whispered, my voice barely audible. A thousand thoughts rushed through my mind. I struggled to grasp them.

"Hmm..."

"What...what is it?"

"There are few like it in this world. But I think you already know what it is."

I swallowed, then slowly, ever so slowly, I turned my head. My heart leapt in my chest. It was there, just behind me, looking over my shoulder. A rush of adrenaline dumped into my body. My eyes turned to black orbs. The demon's eyes, identical to mine, darted over my face and took note of my appearance. It took a step back, giving me space. I turned on the parapet to face it.

My hands trembled. I clamped my journal closed, squeezing. It took another step back, its wings opening and closing, agitated.

"What...what *are* you?" I managed, my whisper breaking the silence.

The thing before me was so humanoid, it struck me with terror. It didn't have hair, and it had giant, leathery wings. Its skin was blackened, as if burnt. But that was simply its natural color. It wore no clothes, and when my eyes dipped, it had no sexual reproductive anatomy visible.

"I am a princep of hell," it hissed in my mind, *"or, some such equivalent."*

"Can...can you speak out loud?"

"I do not think you wish for me to open my mouth."

The promise of *that* had me shaking my head. No—I did not want that. Not at all.

My eyes darted towards the rooftop door, towards safety, before looking back at it.

Dark laughter filled my mind—it was laughing at me. *"I won't harm you, if that is your concern. Unless you try that thing you did before, and then I will promptly stop your heart in your chest."*

My mouth dropped open. "You...you can do that?"

"Can't you? I've seen you work on my kind."

"Yes, but I'm human."

Its head tilted, regarding me. *"Are you?"*

My mouth snapped shut. When it grinned, I saw its razor sharp teeth, protruding behind its gray lips. It saw me staring at them, and its grin grew wider.

"With blood we shed, with blood we keep..."

I gasped. "Those are the words."

"Ahh, yes. You've seen them now."

"I didn't see all of them. What are they?"

"Would you like the whole of it?"

I hesitated, then nodded.

The princep waited a moment, as if expecting me to change my mind, then began to chant.

> *With blood we shed,*
> *with blood we keep,*
> *with blood we guard the blackness deep.*
> *For blood we have,*
> *and blood we give,*
> *we sacrifice so others live.*
> *But when blood fails,*
> *and darkness freed,*
> *the price is life.*
> *So ends our creed.*

I blinked, coldness seeping into my bones. *"Whose* creed? What does it mean."

"Whose do you think—?"

Crack.

The door to the roof burst open, and Rixon stood in the door-way, eyes fearful. I turned, but the demon was gone. Only a distant sound of flapping wings told me I hadn't imagined the whole thing.

Rixon came straight for me, glancing between my face and the journal in my lap. His concern cleared, and he took my chin in his fingers, tilting my face up, looking down at me. "It was here, wasn't it?"

I nodded.

His jaw clenched. "Did it hurt you?"

"No. It...it said it wouldn't. I'm all right, I promise."

Something flashed across his features. It took effort on his part, but he didn't press the matter. Instead, he pivoted. "I've been looking for you. My father's wretched council meeting let out an hour ago and I need you to calm me down before I stab someone, preferably Lord Holland."

A grin replaced my irritation at his interruption. "That bad, hmm?"

"Worse. But I'll spare you the details. Mina—" he hesitated. "Why don't we just leave this place. Leave it all behind."

I got to my feet, studying him. "You're that frightened of it? Of the room below?" His throat bobbed. He didn't need to answer. I saw it clearly in his gaze. Even so many days later.

"It's a portal to hell," I told him.

He flinched. "And who told you that? Your demon friend?"

"It's not my *demon friend*," I said, voice serious. "And, yes. Rixon, something is going on here. And...I don't know if your father knows what it is, or if it's more to do with the keepers, being that we found it beneath the library. But..."

He swore under his breath. "*But*, you want to get to the bottom of it."

I took a deep breath. "We swore an oath, *Lord Wielder*."

"I'm aware, *Lady Witch*. But that oath didn't include things relating to demon portals. This kind of information is for the Citadel—the council."

And yet...I just couldn't let it go. He saw that, clear as day.

"Fucking fuck!" he hissed. "*Mina*." I didn't respond. He took a step back, raking his hands through his hair until it looked wild and unruly, just like him. His eyes looked skyward, as if there'd be answers there. "*Fuuuuck!*" he hissed again, fists tightening, arms flexing. The vein in his neck pulsed erratically.

I watched him, hiding my amusement. When his gaze returned to mine, I said, "Are you quite done with your temper tantrum, Lord Wielder?"

He took a deep inhale, then closed the distance between us. Seconds later, my scalp smarted. He wasn't gentle as he twisted his fingers into my hair, wrenched my head back. His mouth claimed mine. Warmth dropped straight into my belly. I groaned into the wetness of his kiss.

Never mind that we filled our spare moments with an excess of sex. Rixon had a way of claiming me with a simple act that made everything feel new and unexplored. And yet, I knew the taste of his tongue as it invaded my mouth, recognized it as deeply as I recognized my own name.

I collapsed into him, submitting. There was always this. No matter how stressful our lives became, we had *this*.

He pulled me tight in his arms. His erection pressed against my stomach. When his lips moved away, his next words curled something deep in my belly. "I'm going to fuck you right here, Mina, against this parapet overlooking the city. I want the world at your feet while my cock is buried in your cunt.

My chest rose and fell, faster and faster. I stayed rooted in place, gaping at him. A heady mix of something dark and oily dumped into my system, racing outward from my soul, crackling through my veins, like the strike of a match, swallowing up dry wood. Rixon's pupils dilated, drenched with desire. His gaze roved over my face, observing my reaction. A haughty smirk pulled at the corners of his lips.

He snatched me up, planting my hips on the battlement between two crenellations. His movements were erratic, desperate. There were no soft touches, no whispered words of love as he *took* what he wanted, hiking my gown up around my hips, roughly forcing my legs apart, wrapping them about his waist. I gasped, grabbing hold of the crenellations on either side of me.

He pressed two fingers inside me, once, twice, a low growl building at the wetness he found. I cried out, core clenching tight. His free hand fussed with the ties of his pants until his cock sprang free. He wrapped one hand around the back of my neck, possessive, while the other guided the head of his thick length up and down my opening, spreading my wetness. I tried to angle my hips upward, desperate to feel the crown of him at my clit. He tutted, the sound scolding. With a single thrust, he buried himself.

I cried out, from pain, from pleasure, from surprise.

His skin smacked against mine, our mouths clashing. Each breath from my chest was a desperate drag. But he gave me exactly what he promised. He fucked me, each stroke relentless, each stroke tightening my core. I trembled against him.

"Well, Mina? Am I not a man of my word?" he demanded, voice rough.

"Y-yes," I managed, breathless.

"Look at it, Lady Witch," he demanded. "Look at Corinna, the world at your feet."

Gasping at the feel of his cock, stroking against the deepest parts of me, I turned my head slightly. There it was, the mass of buildings, people going about their day, oblivious to the sight far, far above. The sight of their prince fucking his lady witch.

A low, needy moan built in my chest—

"Yes, you like that don't you, little witch? You like what only I can give you—say it."

"Yes. On-only you—"

A loud gasp punctuated our erratic breathing. I tightened up, eyes darting behind Rixon's shoulder. Trudy Holland stood in the doorway.

"Rixon," I gasped.

His thrusts continued, speeding up, turning frenzied, almost painful. But his head turned just a fraction, enough to catch sight of his betrothed. A low chuckle built in his chest. He faced forward again, eyes finding mine.

His expression said everything.

He didn't care that she was watching us with wide eyes, mouth hanging open, hand clutched on the doorframe. And...neither did I. I didn't care that she saw my inner demon, laid bare on the surface of my skin. Didn't care about anything but the ache between my legs.

Rixon's hips retreated, then slammed back into me, pelvic bone grinding against my clit. I blinked, crying out, my voice pleasure-drenched. Uncontrollable shivers spreading across my skin. Together, we raced toward the promise dangling just out of reach. Inside me, the dark presence surged to the surface, bearing an intense sense of freedom. Wings spread wide, it soared through me. I cried out, gasping, as my body clenched up.

I combusted.

Rixon watched my orgasm, eyes fixed on my face in fascination. "Yes, Lady Witch. *Give it to me,*" he bit out the words through clenched teeth. "Every fucking drop. Milk me. Take it all." Little beads of sweat prickled his temples. He threw his head back and roared my name, neck muscles bulging. I clung to him, spasms still wracking my body, the rest of the world forgotten. It didn't matter that it was spread beneath my feet. The only thing that mattered was the man between my legs. The cock buried inside me.

When my breathing steadied, I came back to myself. I looked behind us, towards the doorway. It was empty. I could almost convince myself I'd imagined it. But no, she'd been there— Rixon's betrothed. Something surged, something that had been festering for days. Poisonous thoughts I'd been ignoring, breaking free of captivity. Perhaps I should have felt fear, or even worry. But no, all I felt in that moment was a vindictive sense of satisfaction.

CHAPTER 20

RIXON

Rixon couldn't decide where to look first. The council chamber had been transformed. He clenched his jaw, keeping his feet planted. "Ahh, he's here!" A nasally male voice said, clapping twice. "Everyone, positions! His Highness has arrived so we may begin."

Lady Holland strode over and took up a position by his side. He barely noticed her. Instead, he took stock of his surroundings.

Bolts of fabric lined the far wall—tablecloth choices. A table in the center of the room groaned beneath the weight of nearly twenty flower arrangements. The burst of color was sickening. Another table had party favors. And another, different invitation options. There was also a table against the wall with centerpieces. Even enticing aromas of cooked food, laid out on a wide table overlooked by the kitchen staff, permeated the air with their dinner selections.

"We've been waiting for you," Trudy hissed beside him, face flushed. From anger? Embarrassment? Did he really care which?

It was true, he'd been quite late. She knew why. She'd come to find him when he'd gone searching for Mina. Instead of coming straight here, as he was supposed to do, he'd made his priorities too clear.

"Well, I'm here now," he drawled, shrugging. "Let's get this over with." Without waiting for her answer, he strode to the first table. Invitations. They were spread out to show off intricately scrolling fonts and foil.

The calligrapher stood behind the table, hands clasped, proud. "Hello, Your Highness. Here we have an—"

"That one," he said, pointing to one, without having looked at any.

"Oh, but of course, Your Highness. That one highlights the use of florals—"

"It will do."

He walked off, ignoring Trudy's small gasp in his wake. A few seconds later, her scrambling feet caught up. He stopped at the displays of fabric swatches. A female stood, overseeing the arrangements of wedding colors.

"Your Highness. It is an honor. I have selected several combinations that will make a fine event, showcasing the romance of—"

"There. That one. But remove the purple." He motioned towards a selection at the end.

"But that's—" Trudy's surprised voice.

"Black and white. I'm aware."

"But—"

"That one," he said again through gritted teeth, this time picking up the color swatches of silk, pulling the purple free, then handing what remained to the female before him. She gazed at it open-mouthed. He walked away before anyone could protest—not that they would.

The next table—centerpieces. He picked the ugliest one, making modifications to it until it looked altogether disappointing, removing the little flowers until there was only a single white sprig. He handed it to the designer.

"Aleksander," Trudy hissed, her face turning splotchy. She whispered an apology to the centerpiece designer before racing after him. "Aleksander, *stop this.*"

"You will address me as Your Highness," he said, turning his gaze upon her. They weren't married, and he despised hearing that name. He strode forward and stopped at the next table. Flower bouquets. "None of these are suitable," he said to the florist, making very little show in looking them over.

"You're...Your Highness!" Trudy demanded, lifting her voice this time. He finally stopped, took a good look at her face. Frustrated tears glittered in her eyes. He studied her a moment, then took a deep breath. "Please," she added.

Something in his chest tightened.

He sighed, turning to the occupants in the room. "Leave us. All of you." Their gulps were audible, but the entire planning staff rushed away.

"Is this about earlier?" she demanded, wiping her eyes on her sleeve. "I didn't mean to...to...*see* that. I understand that this marriage, that we, that you will be king and are entitled to bed whomever you wish. That this is just a formality."

His breaths came faster and faster, the severity of the situation crashing down around him. It was too much. He'd done everything Mina had asked of him. He'd played her game, stringing this poor woman along to appease his father. Here she stood, helpless, sputtering, staring at him without a notion of what she was tangled up in.

Guilt dropped into his belly.

He took a deep breath and said, "Surely you know there will be no wedding."

Her mouth snapped shut before her brow furrowed. "Is this...is this about your lady witch? Your father said that she would cooperate. I understand if you love her, but we—"

"No, Lady Holland." He squeezed the bridge of his nose, tilting his head back. It was entirely unfair, all of this. And Trudy Holland, as irritating as she was, was innocent. "Let me make something very clear. I love Mina more than I love anything in this world. I would die for her—a thousand times over. I would burn the entire fucking world to see her happy." Trudy Holland's eyes rounded, still glittering with unshed tears. "There will be no wedding."

"But...but I've been *waiting*. Ten years, since the arrangements were made. I waited for you," she managed.

He winced, closing his eyes. "Whatever my father promised you, was not his to promise. Lady Holland, you deserve someone who can love you, cherish you. The fact that you are okay with this," he waved a hand to encompass the room, "while simultaneously giving me permission to take lovers, is not acceptable. Can you not see that? I am not the person for you."

"This is a *royal wedding*," she said, chest rising and falling. "I never deluded myself that love would be part of it."

"Then you are cheating yourself."

"But—but we are to be married. Your father made the announcement to the entire court. You...you have gone along with it, agreed upon a date, everything."

He sighed, looking her over. "That was unfair of me. I will speak to my father about it, if I must."

Her face changed. A low, deranged laugh bubbled up in her chest. "Very well. But I will say this. Your father will not be quick to relinquish the agreement, not when my father's Nebrine mines are in question."

He hid his surprise and nodded.

Trudy Holland gave him a final look and departed, leaving him alone in a room filled with the reminder of what he'd just done.

"Fuck!" he hissed, looking down at the flower bouquets before him. He growled, and in a moment of weakness, struck out, sweeping them from the table. Vases shattered. Water spilled across the floor. "Fuck!" he shouted, this time, digging his fingers into his hair.

Mina would be furious. What would he say to her? How would he face her?

He took a deep, steadying breath, getting his emotions under control. Then he squared his shoulders and left the room, not sparing a single glance for the attendants lining the walls, waiting to return to their display tables.

His father was tense at the dinner table, hand gripping his goblet. The table arrangement hadn't changed. The Hollands sat across from him. Mina was on his left. He shot a glance in her direction, hating that she wouldn't meet his gaze. She'd been furious when he'd returned to their room and broke the news. So furious, that she'd walked out without a single word. He hadn't missed the way her eyes had blackened with rage.

He'd tried to follow after her, but she'd used the bond on him, keeping him trapped within the chamber like a child. He'd acted like one, losing his control with Trudy, stepping out of line.

Once Mina had returned, it was removed.

"I'm sorry," was all he'd managed, but her silence didn't break.

They'd gone down to dinner, the tension between them palpable. There'd been times of tension before, but never quite like this. He hated it—felt sick to his stomach. He should have discussed his rash decision before simply ending things with Trudy. Before risking their safety.

Now a million scenarios played out, each as awful as the next, about how his father would punish him. How he would lash out against Mina. How he would change the game.

Lord Holland's eyes darted between Rixon and the king, as if waiting for the king to publicly scold his son. That didn't happen. He almost wished it would. Almost wanted his father to make a scene so that he might lash out in some way.

Instead, the meal was hushed. Even the king's guests felt the tension. Mina simply ignored him. He pushed food around on his plate but didn't eat anything.

At last, when the dessert was cleared away, they retreated. The moment their door shut behind them, he spun towards her. "Talk to me, Lady Witch. Don't freeze me out anymore."

"Talk to you? And tell you what, precisely? Tell you how careless you've been? How your little stunt put both our lives in danger?!"

He swallowed.

Mina walked across the room, then spun back towards him, her expression wrathful. "I half expected the king to arrest me at dinner. Imagine what a scene! What would you have done then, hm? Fought off his guards? Harmed innocent people? Because *that's* what it would have come to, Rixon."

She huffed, shaking her head. "The thing inside me would have taken over. I would have fought them off with my magic. And *then* what?"

He turned cold. If it had happened that way, everyone would have discovered her secret. She'd have been forced to flee. Word sent to the Citadel. Witches hunting her, believing her a demon. The scenario terrified him.

Her chest rose and fell with agitation.

"I'm sorry," he managed again, opening and closing his hands. "I lost control."

"Yes, I'm aware. I should have been more creative with my leash," she hissed. He flinched. Her eyes squeezed shut, and she managed to get control of herself. "I'm sorry. I shouldn't have said it that way."

He exhaled. "I deserve it."

"This decision you've made, Rixon, it will not go unpunished. The king will strike, and he will strike hard. I certainly hope that whatever happens, was worth your moment of weakness."

He scrubbed a hand over his face. "I did what I thought was right, Mina. I got tangled in the heat of the moment."

"What was right?" she muttered, beginning to pace again. "What was right?"

"It wasn't fair," he clarified. "This ruse."

She spun on her heel. "Oh, yes. Poor Trudy. Innocent Trudy. I bet she's not as innocent as you think. Moreover, this is a dangerous game we're playing, Rixon. You know that! Trudy Holland's discomfort is not worth our lives."

Rixon winced. "It won't come to that, Lady Witch."

She laughed. The sound of it sent chills down his spine. It wasn't entirely her laugh, either. "Your life, perhaps, is safe. Mine is worthless. You're the only one he needs."

"Mina..." He took a step towards her, then hesitated as she threw out a hand to stop him. Not with magic, just with a gesture.

She closed her eyes and started muttering to herself. Something about how stupid she'd been, to believe this would be easy, to believe she could have bested his father.

"Mina."

She continued to mutter.

"*Lady Witch*," he finally demanded, interrupting her.

She opened her eyes, still tight with anger. "I can't be here right now."

He frowned.

She crossed the room and wrenched the door open.

"Where are you going?" he demanded. She froze in the doorway, turning to look at him over her shoulder.

"For a walk. Away from *you*, you infuriating—"

"Mina," he begged.

"It's just a walk, Rixon." Something in his expression made hers soften a measure.

"I don't like you going off alone," he managed. "Especially not right now."

She sighed, her shoulders somewhat relaxing. "I need space, Rixon. I need...to be alone. I won't go far—to the garden. But I need to be away from you right now."

He flinched, then nodded. "Of...of course," he said, ignoring the ache in his chest.

Her eyes fluttered shut; she was mastering herself. When they next opened, they were normal again. She stepped into the hall-way. He watched her go, his insides twisting with shame. She'd never been so disappointed in him. He needed to fix this.

Seconds ticked by. He stood motionless, in thoughtful consid-eration, then he strode from the room, shutting their door and continuing on through the palace. When he entered the kitchen, the room fell silent. Cooks and servants were cleaning up after dinner. Upon seeing who had entered, they began bowing. "What can I get for you, Your Highness?"

"Chocolate," he said to the head cook.

"Chocolate, Prince Aleksander?"

"Yes, as much as you can."

"But, Your Highness, we only have the ingredients. We would need to make some. That could take thirty minutes. More."

He sighed. "I'll wait."

"Very well." The head cook motioned to several assistants. They jumped into action. As he sat there, his mind wandered. He had half a mind to take the chocolate in its melted form and pour it all over her tight body and lick it off. Perhaps that would reduce her ire towards him?

His center clenched. He pushed the thought from his mind, leaning back against the trestle tables as he waited. For the first few minutes, everyone scuttling around gave him a wide berth, but after a time, they relaxed.

All too soon, the smell of chocolate filled the room. He breathed it in, watching the cooks work, stirring the chocolate concoction over the stove in pots, then pouring it into molds. One of them turned to him. "It should only need about twenty minutes to cool, Your Highness." He merely nodded, leaning back further against the table, letting his long legs splay out, crossing his arms.

A few of the female servants glanced his way and blushed.

He spent the remaining time thinking about how he'd win Mina over. Chocolate, obviously. More whispered apologies. A back massage would help, and he'd make it the best damned massage she'd ever had. Orgasms were on the table, certainly—

"There you are, Your Highness. Will this be enough?" The cook began stacking bricks of milk chocolate on layers of parchment paper.

"That's plenty," he said. More than plenty. Far too much. But knowing his Mina, she'd find a way to consume it. He hid the twitch of his lips, thanking the cooks, then gathering up the bundle and returning to their room.

How long had he been gone? Nearly an hour? She was probably back now, and he braced himself for the mood she'd be in, hoping her walk had calmed her down. He entered, slamming the door with his foot. "I hope you're ready for some chocolate. I've enough to last you two weeks—"

He frowned, gaze darting around the empty room. "Mina?"

His stomach dropped. Her shoes and cloak were still missing. He set the chocolate down and moved about the room, pouring a large glass of wine to be ready upon her return. Then he tracked down a bottle of massage oil. Minutes ticked by, and still she did not return.

Frowning, he went to the window, looking down into the gardens. The torches flickered below, but he saw no signs of movement. Was she already on her way up? He stood...and waited. Minute after minute ticked by, until a growing sense of fear took hold of him.

"Fuck," he hissed. He backed away from the window. Glancing down at himself, he made sure his weapons were belted in place. Then he strode from the room in search of his lady witch.

CHAPTER 21

MINA

I meandered through the garden, taking in the flickering torches lining the paths. It was magical at night. Something about the dark shadows kissing the cool air, the flickering torches, and the stars overhead. I'd visited several times during the day, but it never felt quite like this. I adjusted the neck of my tunic, tugging at it.

With each passing day, the thing inside me gained strength. I was more volatile. Quicker to anger. Rixon's mistake had been an honest one, albeit careless.

I took a deep breath, slowly exhaling. What a mess. Everything was spiraling out of my control. Today, especially, had been an absolute disaster.

We were no closer to solving the demon problem and now I wondered if we could. With all that had happened, could I continue playing the king's games? Or was everything ruined.

It wasn't just the broken engagement. It was what Trudy had seen on the roof. She'd found us fucking; she'd seen my demon crazed eyes. Part of that was Rixon's doing. I was all too aware that he'd gone in search of me, knowing she had been looking for him, knowing she'd find him on the roof. Maybe he'd done it in hopes of her backing out on their engagement. When she hadn't, he'd taken matters into his own hands.

Was I entirely blameless? No. I could have stopped us immediately, hidden my face from view. Instead, I'd looked at her, challenged her as she stood there gaping at us. Let her see how much I enjoyed him.

It was shallow, my jealousy.

A small part of me—a sliver that was still good—recognized that it wasn't my finest moment. The rest of me—the darker half, the *stronger* half—relished in her discovery. I liked the pain it caused. Rixon belonged to *me*, and me alone. Anyone who believed otherwise deserved whatever misfortune came their way.

I stopped before a hedge of red roses, reaching out to caress an open bud.

The king believed Rixon belonged to him—his *creature* to do with as he pleased. I clenched my fist around the bud, ripping the petals from the stem. His father thought he could *take* him from me, thought he could split us apart.

I opened my hand, letting the petals flutter to the ground—

"They say roses are the flowers of love."

I whirled, coming face to face with King Maddox. He had a contingent of guards flanking him. They fanned out around us. My eyes darted over them as my fist, now empty, clenched and dropped to my side.

"I had these planted for Leone, shortly before we wed." He clasped his hands behind his back, the picture of calm collection. "I loved that woman, even before we married. I was lucky in that. Most marriages are ones of convenience."

I swallowed, calculating.

"She loved them for their beauty," he continued, eyes gazing over the sea of roses. "But beauty can be dangerous, can it not?" He reached out and plucked one by the stem, ignoring the danger of the thorns.

The guards around us shifted, moving about the garden casually. I tracked them in my peripherals, pretending to keep my full attention on Maddox. Inside, I had a well of power waiting, desperate to burst free. I would use it on him if I had to. I would kill every single guard in this garden, if it came down to it.

Hesitating, he handed me the rose. I carefully lifted it to my nose, letting its sweet fragrance wash over me, letting it ground me. My eyes stayed locked on his. The king had loved his wife —I knew that much.

Perhaps it was the one thing that made him likable.

"When she died, I was...undone," he explained. "I had the royal gardeners fill the entire garden with them, roses in every color. A reminder for what I had lost. Like roses, love is both beauty and pain."

It was almost uncanny how much of Rixon's face I saw in him. Frightening, really. But there was no mistaking the decay present. He was wasting away. Sick.

"I heard from Miss Holland this afternoon, that my son has seen fit to break his engagement. I realize now that perhaps love is to blame. That perhaps he has the same kind of love I once had, the kind that claims you, the kind that breaks you." His gaze hardened. "The kind that controls you."

Ice slipped into my belly. I dug deeper into my well, a cat ready to pounce. Around us, the world remained frozen, ready to shatter.

"I was mistaken to believe I could remove you from the picture, Lady Witch." At his admission, I blinked. "My son loves you. Only a blind fool would miss it. And so, I have made a new realization." My heart thumped. "He cannot lose you."

My lips parted. Was this...a trick? A new game?

"He cannot lose you, but neither can he have you—" His fingers flicked.

A bow twanged. My eyes went wide, pain exploding through my middle. My mouth opened in a silent gasp. I staggered back, looking down. The head of an arrow protruded from my belly. *Twang. Twang. Twang.* More pain exploded all over me. In my chest, my arm, my thigh. A split second later, I took a gasping breath, releasing my torrent of magic, to protect me, to save me, to obliterate everything in this garden—

Nothing happened.

I hiccuped, falling, knees slamming against the cobbled path as I drilled down, pulling. An animalistic sound rose in my throat, eyes blackening, veins spreading across my skin. It was there. I could *feel* it, within reach. I gulped down another drag of air, clawing at the arrows. It was fire—agony. Every subtle movement made me hiss.

Unwittingly, I looked up at the king, my eyes blurred. A tear broke free, slipping down the corner of my cheek. Was this really where he planned to kill me? But...he'd said...

The king stood there, watching my struggle, his lips flat. It was the gaze of a victor. "I find Nebrine to be quite useful against demons."

"*No!*" I managed to hiss, the word barely audible. I pulled at the arrow in my center, trying to wrench it free. The edges of my vision darkened. *Twang.* Another. This time, I fell face forward, catching myself on my hands. The last thought in my mind was of Rixon. Of how much I loved him, of what our last words had been, of what my death would do to him.

Then everything went black.

I wasn't dead—my first thought. I swallowed, my throat sandpaper dry. My tongue caught on the roof of my mouth. I worked it until moisture returned. My awareness followed. Groaning, I flopped over, nuzzled into the blankets, looking for the feel of Rixon's warmth—

I jerked upright. Everything in me ached, the echoes of pain still singing through me. I scrambled backwards, until my back struck a solid wall. The surroundings of a cell came in and out of focus.

Everything rushed back and my breath quickened. "No..." I croaked, voice rough. "No!" I lifted my hands, searching for arrow wounds, but they were already healed.

My wrists clanked. My eyes widened.

"*Nebrine.*" The hiss on my tongue belongs to a demon. I tugged at the shackles, scrambling from the bed. I dug for my magic, tunneling. A deep well waited, vast and eager, glowing white twined with black, accented by wisps of red. I plummeted all the way to the bottom, until I saw the very essence of what I was—what I had become. Then I pulled.

My stomach swooped. Nausea crawled up my throat. I gasped, trying to release the torrent within me. Only, it slammed against a barrier.

I staggered backward, my knees hitting the bed, falling into a sitting position. "No," I whispered again. "No, no, no!" My limbs shook, unable to sit still, I jumped to my feet again. My mouth opened. I screamed, letting fury wrap around my voice. A voice that didn't sound like my own.

I rushed to the small mirror on the wall, just above a tiny sink. My fingers brushed over my face. It was still mine, mottled with blackened veins. My eyes, black orbs, stared back at me. My hair, dark as night, flowed around me, ethereal, nearly floating.

I made an attempt to calm my breathing, to think rationally. How long had I been here? Rixon would have noticed my absence. I pulled on the bond, tugged hard, signaling as I did with demons.

It resisted, as if...

I looked down at the shackles. A laugh bubbled up from my chest, turning hysterical, manic. He'd figured it out. Somehow, when I hadn't. The king had caged my magic.

"That fucking little..." Trudy had seen what I was, earlier. She'd told the king. I would kill her. When I got free, I would wrap my fingers around her pretty little neck and twist until it snapped—

I blinked, pushing the violent thought out of my mind.

Heaviness settled deep in my limbs. I went to the bars. Nebrine bars. They stood floor to ceiling along the far side of my cell, looking out to a corridor. "Rixon?!" I called. "Hello?"

There was a scuff. A shoe, perhaps. "I am a lady witch of the Citadel," I shouted, letting my voice carry down the empty hallway. "I command you to release me—immediately."

No response.

"Let me out!" I screamed, letting the thing inside me surge to the surface.

Still, nothing.

I began to pace, calculating. The silence pressed in around me. Rixon would discover my absence. He'd come searching for me.

My jaw clenched. I couldn't let it come to that. My wielder was meant to protect me, yes, but I had more magic than any witch in existence. A strangled laugh burst from my chest. Magic that was now warped. Demonic. I slumped down on the bed. My magic...my poor magic. What good would it do me now?

I'd have to rely on something else. I began searching, looking for something sharp, or perhaps something I could use if someone came into my cell. My confines were not what I would have expected. They were comfortable. A plush bed, a small sofa, and table with two chairs off to one side, a sink and toilet on the opposite end. There was a small pile of towels, washcloths, and even...clothes.

"You will find that royalty is treated better than most prisoners."

"You!" I spun, facing the king. He held a covered platter in his hands. My eyes darted over it before returning to his face. "Release me."

"I'm afraid I cannot."

Cannot, or will not? I scoffed. The latter, obviously. My lips curled. "Why are you doing this?"

His head tilted to the side. "I told you before."

"You think you can use my captivity to control Rixon?"

"My son would have razed the palace to the ground, emerging from the ashes with nothing more than vengeance to show for his efforts, had I killed you. As I said, I recalculated once his love became apparent. Here—" He maneuvered the covered platter through the bars, turning it on end before setting it on the ground.

I went to it and kicked it, watching the lid spring free, the contents scatter. "There! *That's* what I think of your fucking recalculations," I spat.

He stood to his full height, face expressionless, gazing at me. "I will allow you that one. But do it again, and you'll simply starve. Tell me, how long can a demon go without food before it craves blood and flesh instead?"

"I am *not* a demon," I hissed, failing even now to hide the sudden change in my voice.

"No? Perhaps not *entirely*. But certainly in part. Admittedly, I am quite curious about you. But if I asked, I doubt I would get the truth."

"You would get *nothing*."

"There. See? Fortunately for us both, you will be down here a long, long time. And by then, you'll be desperate for company, I suspect."

"You think Rixon is going to cooperate with you?"

The king barked a laugh. "He will, when his precious witch is threatened."

"So I was right. You *will* use me to manipulate him," I said, my upper lip curling with disgust. He shrugged. "You're disgust—"

"I have a kingdom to protect, girl. What I protect it from is far more important than my son's love for you."

I stilled. Something in his face, in his words, made me hesitate. He wasn't talking about the kind of protection that came with being a king, ruling a kingdom. He was talking about...something else. He gazed at me, rubbing his gloved thumb along the palm of his hand. I went still. That gesture, that motion—

"My son will not find you down here. You are not in the dungeons used for prisoners. Aleksander was too young when he left to know about this place. In fact, I am the only person in the kingdom who knows of it. Recently, I even had it fitted with Nebrine bars, to accommodate you. I had to kill the builders, unfortunately. I regret that, at least, but sacrifices must be made."

My blood roared through my veins.

"You see, in times past, kings had many heirs, larger families. But, no family is perfect. Our rulers needed a place to keep our...bad apples. Rotten as they might be, they were of the blood, after all, and our blood is important."

I blinked. *Blood*. My body jolted.

"So? This holding cell was built. There is only one way in, and one way out. And unless you know exactly where the entrance is, how to reach it..." He stopped speaking, looking me over. "There will be no escape for you, Lady Witch. But, you have my word, that as long as Aleksander cooperates, you will live a comfortable life. And if you behave, I might just let you see him...on occasion. If I am feeling generous."

"You're a fucking monster," I hissed. His brow lifted, as if mocking the insult. "You're just going to let your people continue to die, picked off by demons night after night?"

"Oh, that." He huffed, waving a hand dismissively. "No, that will be remedied soon enough." I stepped forward, my urge to understand overcoming my hatred. I searched his face, as if I might find answers. But what he said next only confirmed my suspicions. "I am sick, dying. But Aleksander is young and healthy. His blood will be strong. As will be the blood of his heirs, I think."

My stomach lifted into my throat. I opened my mouth—

"You will find, Lady Witch, that I will do anything to save my kingdom from ruin. Scorn me all you wish. Judge me. Hate me. Rail against me. But I do what I must to keep Raeria alive and thriving. I will not have you getting in the way of that. It is either my kingdom's downfall, or yours. I made my decision."

I gaped at him, blinking. He turned, striding out of sight. Rushing to the bars, I wrapped my fingers around them, pressed my face between them. "Come back," I screamed. "Come back you fucking coward! Face me like a real male. Face me without your filthy little tricks—" I broke off, breathing hard, listening. He was gone.

There was only silence.

CHAPTER 22

RIXON

The garden was empty. Rixon's eyes darted over the budding roses, searching the shadows. There was no sign of her. He turned, striding back through the entryway, then paused. "I'm looking for my lady witch," he said to the guards standing at attention just outside the entrance.

"Your Highness," they greeted.

"Have you seen her?"

They shifted. One of them finally said, "She came this way not but fifteen minutes ago, then left in a hurry."

He frowned. "Which way did she go?"

"That way, Prince Aleksander. Towards the palace gates."

"The palace—" He stopped himself, eyes narrowing. "You're sure?"

"Yes, Your Highness," they said, nodding.

He eyed them a moment longer, then turned on his heel and made his way through the palace, towards the portcullis. She wouldn't have left the palace without him…would she?

He stopped off at the stable. Jarrow and Ferrah nickered, greeting him. He gave them each an affectionate pat. "Aleksander!" Kam strode from around the corner. "I wondered if that was you I heard."

"Mina hasn't been this way, has she?"

"Not that I've seen. No one's been through here for a couple of hours. Is…is everything all right?"

His stomach squirmed. "Fine. Forgive me, I need to go."

He went to the gates, already sealed tight for curfew. "Have you seen my lady witch?" he asked the guards on duty.

There was a hesitation, then, "She asked to be let out, Your Highness."

"I thought the gates didn't open after curfew," he demanded. Looks were exchanged. His lips pressed into a line.

Before the nearest guard could open his mouth, he freed a Nebrine blade and pressed it against the guard's neck. "Do not lie to me again. I will cut your fucking throat out. I don't care who you are. I don't care that you're my father's guard." He pressed until the guard's skin began to split. A bead of blood dripped down the guard's neck.

"Tell me true."

"She…went this way," he gasped out, eyes darting.

"Then why don't I believe you?!" He pressed the knife in, watching the guard's skin part further.

"Please, Your Highness," another said.

"Silence," he hissed at them, turning back to the male at his mercy. "Give me the truth. Did she, or did she not pass this way? Did you open the gates for her? Do not lie, or I will know."

"We opened the gates for her ten minutes ago—at her insistence. She...she threatened us with magic. With..." The guard shook his head, unable to give an answer.

He'd lied to the guard. He had no way of discerning the truth. Only a gut feeling. And in this instance, he really couldn't tell.

His eyes darted back towards the place, then to the portcullis, sealed tight. She would have signaled him with the bond, if something was wrong, wouldn't she? Perhaps she was angrier than he'd imagined.

His throat constricted. He stepped back, sheathing the blade. "Open the gate."

"Your...Your highness?"

"I said, open the *fucking* gate."

They jumped into action. He ducked under it before it had completely lifted, striding to the first place that came to mind. The *King's Mantle* came into view. He ducked inside and spoke to the hostess. "She hasn't come this way, Lord Wielder, I'd have known. Everyone checks in with me upon entry." His stomach lurched.

"Rixon?" Elianna appeared, a shall wrapped tight around her shoulders. She stood in the archway of the sitting room. "Where's Mina?"

He tried to answer. His mouth opened, then closed. Not a word emerged.

"She didn't come with you?"

He gave a shake of his head. Something was...something was *wrong*. Elianna must have sensed it. She called for Viktor, then guided Rixon out of the inn, onto the porch. "Tell me," she urged.

"We...we had a little disagreement. She was upset with me. She went walking in the garden, so I went in search of...of chocolate."

"Chocolate?!" Elianna gave a small laugh. "All right."

"She's...she's gone."

"Perhaps she just needed some time to clear her—"

"No," he insisted, his voice lifting. "No."

Viktor shifted closer to his witch, eying him.

He sighed. "She wouldn't leave without telling me. The guards, they said she left the palace, but...no."

"You think they were lying?"

His mind flashed over possibility after possibility. "I don't know," he said at last. His fear made him too frantic, jumbling his thoughts, making it hard to rationalize. "Perhaps she went into the tunnels."

"The tunnels?" Eliaanna's brows pulled together.

He quickly told her about them. What they'd found. Even about the strange room near the library's archives.

"Why don't we help you search? I know there's curfew and all, but...I don't like this," Elianna said. "Not one bit."

He gave a curt nod.

"Is it all right if Anne joins us, too? She's a wicked good witch, despite her talkative manner."

He hesitated. "All right, but no more than that. I don't want to deal with guards tonight."

Elianna slipped back inside. Viktor was a silent presence as they waited. A few minutes later, Anne emerged, Ronan with her. The five of them left the inn, keeping to the shadowed side streets.

"Keep your eyes open," he said, feeling suddenly vulnerable. Mina's ability to sense demons had softened him. Without her, they needed to remain alert.

They spoke little as he led them to the river, to the entry into the tunnels. "You're sure it is safe to enter, Lord Wielder?" Elianna asked, hesitating.

"Mina and I have spent many nights down here," he said, lifting the torch he'd grabbed along the way. "You can see the letters she's etched into some of the walls, if you don't believe me."

"This isn't some ploy to question us further about the demons —you don't truly suspect us, do you?" Anne said, eying him.

"Fucking gods above," he hissed. "My lady witch is missing. I don't give a shit about demons right now—except that you should kill them, if we find any."

With that, he turned and entered the tunnels, the others on his heels. He searched, calling for her, following the Ms until they reached the library archives. He led them to the strange octagonal room.

"She's not here," he said, his chest clenching. It had been a last ditch effort, a small hope that something had drawn her here. A quick glance towards the arch on the fall wall showed fresh blood, still dripping, smeared over its surface. The wall did not waver, and his companions did not ask about it. They stood just outside, waiting.

A strange urge led him to the dungeons next. Silently, they crept past cells, eying each one. Some were occupied, but none of them held Mina. His fear mounted.

Hours passed, and when she did not turn up, he led them back to the inn. "Perhaps she's simply back at the palace, waiting for you," Anne said, her voice encouraging. "This whole thing might just be a mix up." Both witches looked exhausted. Their wielders shifted, hands on the pommels of their *Nebrine* swords, silent.

All he could do was nod, before bidding them goodnight. When he returned to the palace, he demanded entry. It was denied. So he sat down, right there against the palace walls, surrounded by dread, shaking from head to toe, and waited.

The moment the portcullis opened, Rixon stormed the palace. He'd had hours to think, to consider, to draw several very obvious conclusions. He went straight to his father's chambers.

The sun hadn't quite crested the horizon, and many of the corridors were still dark. Servants rushed about, preparing for the day. They shot him wary glances as he passed, covered in tunnel muck, a hard look on his face.

He reached the two guards at his father's door. They stepped before it, hands tight on their spears. "Your High—"

"Step aside," he growled, keeping his voice low.

"Your father is still readying for the—"

Faster than they could blink, he pulled a Nebrine blade , taking the left guard by his tunic, pressing the sharp edge against his throat. The guard's face paled. The other shifted uncomfortably, lifting his spear, uncertain. "If you don't step the fuck aside right now, I will cut your fucking throat, take the key from your ring, and open it myself."

The guard's throat bobbed. He gave a shaky nod. Rixon released him. The guard's hands trembled as he fussed with his ring, then slipped the key into the lock, opening the door that led to the king's private apartments.

He gave the guards a final look then strode inside. He'd only been in here the one time since his return, with Mina. "Aleksander," his father said, pushing away from the dining table, away from his breakfast. The king's attendants glanced between them, wary. "A little early for a visit, don't you think?"

"Where is she?!" he roared, striding across the room. "You sent me on a fucking wild goose chase last night so you could get your claws in her. If you so much as put a scratch on her skin, so help me, I will rip your fucking throat out."

He ignored the gasps.

The king did not. "Leave us," he said to his attendants. They gathered their papers and supplies, leaving their breakfast discarded, and rushed from the room.

"Where is she?" he said again, hand clenched on the hilt of his blade. "What did you do to her?"

"Relax. She's here. Unharmed—mostly. A little angry, obviously."

A muscle above his eye began to twitch. "Where the fuck is she?" he said again, taking a step forward.

"I put her somewhere safe. Somewhere no one can touch her, least of all you."

"I will tear this fucking palace apart—"

"And yet, you still won't find her." It was a bluff–had to be. His father liked playing games.

"Now, we're going to need to work on that temper of yours, boy. A good king doesn't wear his emotions on his sleeve, no matter the cost. We have a great deal of work to do in a very short—"

His vision went red. He closed the distance between them, dragging his father by the tunic, slamming him against the wall. The point of his blade came to rest at the base of his father's throat. He could only think of one thing. How badly he wanted to drive the blade through that soft flesh and out the other side.

"I *hated* you as a child," he growled, the words rushing out before he could stop them. Words that were long overdue. Words he finally had the courage to say. "All I ever wanted was your approval, your acceptance. All I ever got were harsh reprimands. Nothing was ever good enough for you. But I was weak. Instead of letting it go, I tried harder and harder, until finally, I couldn't take it anymore and left. I have spent the last fifteen years running from you, but no more. I would love nothing more than to kill you."

"Really, Aleksander. We both know you haven't got it in you. You never did."

"If you do not tell me where she is, I will drive this blade straight through your throat."

The king huffed. "Then you will never find her."

"Then I will torture the information from you," he roared.

The door behind him burst open. The king's guards strode in, spears raised, awaiting orders. "Leave us," the king barked. "And see that no one enters. Kill them if they try."

Both guards left.

"That," Rixon said, "was a mistake." He wrapped his fingers around his father's throat, pulled the blade back, and drove it into his father's shoulder instead, careful to avoid a lethal blow. The king grunted, eyes going wide. That look of surprise was the sweetest revenge he'd ever felt.

"You didn't think I'd do it, did you?" he growled. "Now, tell me where she is?!"

The king's mouth worked, opening and closing. He removed the blade, ignoring the sound it made, and drove it into his father's thigh, next. This time, the king made a strangled grunt, laced with pain.

"I will keep going," he warned. "I will do what I've imagined doing for years. *I will make you suffer.*"

"Aleks...Aleksander..." It was a warning. Even now, his father was trying to *scold* him, to warn him to behave.

"I'll make sure you bleed out on the carpet—right here."

"Aleksander..."

"There is only *one* person in this palace who can heal you now. Take me to her, and she will heal you. Refuse, and I'll let you drop dead right here."

"Aleksander...If I die..." the king managed, "you doom all of Raeria. They will...they will break through and *decimate* us."

He froze. Chills spread over his skin. Battle scenes flashed through his mind—hordes of demons, thousands of them, facing off before the legions of the king's armies, on a battle-field littered with bodies. "What did you say?"

"There's a...a doorway," his father continued. "A room... under...the library."

"The mural room." His throat went dry. He pressed his father harder against the wall, keeping him upright.

"You've...you've seen it then..." The king took a deep, ragged breath, then nodded to himself. "Yes. It has...has been guarded for centuries."

"By whom?" Rixon demanded.

"Whom do you...think?" his father managed. Rixon's blood turned to ice. "By...by me...my father...my father's father. Generations of Kozmas. Our blood...it responds...to our blood. We...are the guardians. Together...the guardians...and the keepers...keep the way...shut. I...I tested your blood, as...as a child."

His hand itched—the scar. The deep gash Mina had noticed not so long ago. He resisted the urge to itch it. His eyes darted downward, to his father's gloved hands. Keeping him pressed against the wall, he reached out and removed the glove on his left hand. His eyes widened.

It was bandaged, white gauze already bleeding. "I tried...I tried the blood of my bastard children. It...did not work. Only yours...you are...my heir."

"The blood on the archway—it's yours?"

"I'm dying, Aleksander."

"Then take me to Mina," he demanded, "and she will heal—"

"No!" the king hissed. "I mean, I'm *dying*. Look at me. I'm... sick. The portal...it takes its toll...in time. I cannot...not for much longer."

"That's why you needed me back here? You fucking piece of shit. You orchestrated everything to bring me back, didn't you?"

"Demons were already...slipping through. By ones and twos. Giving less blood...it made the portal...weaker. Allowed more to slip...through."

"Take me to Mina," Rixon growled.

The king's eyes began losing clarity. "You have always been honorable, Aleksander. In that, at least, I admire you—even if your honor was, perhaps, misplaced. I...I cannot give you what you want, unless you give me what I need."

A loud, furious growl rose in his chest. "And what is it, then, that you *need*?" His patience was wearing thin. If his father died here, before showing him the way, it might mean never finding Mina.

"I...will make a deal with you," the king offered, his voice strengthening.

"What sort of deal?" he said, growing wary. But did it matter? His father was dying, bleeding out on the carpet, and there wasn't time. Besides, he had a feeling he already knew exactly what his father would say.

With broken words, the king laid out everything he wanted.

CHAPTER 23

MINA

There was a battlefield, and demons, thousands...tens of thousands...spread before me. The air smelled like iron, thick and oppressive. Just like the armor shielding my body. *Nebrine* armor. It weighed me down like a burden, suppressing the thing inside me. Shackling me.

But I needed it, the protection. I needed it for what we were about to face. *The blackness deep.* It was here. We had failed, somehow. The darkness, it was free, seeping into the world, snuffing it out, strangling the heartbeat of the living.

The witches, the Citadel—we had failed to protect the people of this kingdom. There were too few of us. Too few to conquer the tidal wave sweeping through our kingdom. We had failed Raeria, and now, the price was the lives of our people. We could only face the darkness as a kingdom, and hope to come out alive.

"Mina!"

I turned to Rixon at my side. He stood in shining armor like mine, shoulders back, face grim, ready for what was to come. And beyond us, pennants whipped in the wind, the crests of noble families. I blinked again. My eyes widened. It wasn't Rixon beside me. No, it was...it was his *father*, crowned, atop a white battle horse.

"*Mina!*" My name again.

I gasped, bolting upright, dragging down air like a drowning person. My arms lifted, ready to protect myself from a sea of demons. I blinked, and my cell came in and out of focus. My hands dropped as I gathered my bearings.

"Mina!" Pounding footsteps.

I shot out of bed. "Rixon?!" I screamed, my voice dry from disuse. "Rixon! Down here!"

He'd found me! Even despite what the king had said, somehow, he'd found me. I let out a huge breath.

My wielder. My rock. The male I loved—would do anything to protect—had found me.

The footsteps grew louder, and then he was there, skidding to a halt before my cell, a bloodied body cradled against him. A—

"Hurry!" he hissed, eyes darting over me, assessing, ensuring I was whole. "We haven't got much time. Heal him."

I staggered back, shock, even confusion, coursing through me. He lowered his father's body to the ground, crouching beside him. A knife protruded from the king's leg. Blood seeped from his shoulder, soaking his tunic red. He looked dead, save for a subtle rise and fall of his chest.

"Save him, Mina." Rixon looked at me, eyes hard. His breaths were quick and shallow, panicked. I'd rarely seen him like this. "Mina—"

My nostrils flared. Something dark settled inside me. "No." The single word fell from my mouth like a hammer upon an anvil. With it, something surged deep within me, pleased. If the king died, so be it.

"Mina, I—"

"*No!*"

"I know what this looks like, and I'll explain everything. The portal. The blood. The blackness deep." I jolted, then blinked, coming back to myself, clamping down on my dark thoughts. "He knows what it is, Mina. He's been guarding it, protecting Raeria, but there's no time. I need him *alive*."

My insides turned to ice. The dream I'd just had flashed through my mind. I knew. In that instant—I *knew*. Still, I hesitated, crouched on the floor, looking over the king's body. He'd lost so much blood. Already, his organs were shutting down, his body lapsing into a coma. Any minute, his heart would fail. I opened my mouth—

"Mina! *Save him!*" Rixon demanded, his voice strangled.

"Rix...I...I *can't*." My voice cracked.

"This isn't about your revenge—"

"No! I mean—" I lifted my wrists, displaying my shackles. Never mind the bars. "I cannot *save* him, Rix," I cried, eyes darting between Rixon's shocked expression and the half-dead king on the ground.

"*Nebrine* shackles?!" he hissed, making the realization. My heart sped up, pulse roaring in my ears. He looked down at his father, eyes blinking rapidly. "Where is the key?!" he demanded, shaking the king, as if he might open his eyes and tell him.

I sagged, looking over the pathetic scene before me. Getting me out of the cell was one thing. Removing the shackles was another matter entirely. Hunting down the key would take time, precious time we did not have.

Blood pooled on the stones, seeping out of King Kozma's shoulder. "The other witches," I blurted, jumping to my feet, gripping the cold bars with my hands. "Elianna, Anna. They might be able to heal him, Rix, enough to keep him alive."

It was a mere possibility. A hope. Rixon's lips parted, brows drawing together.

"Go!" I cried. "If you want to save him. He has minutes—if you're lucky. *Go!*"

Rixon nodded, eyes distant, then gathered up his father and sprinted away. I listened to his receding footsteps until they faded entirely. Silence fell. I staggered back to my cot, sinking down onto it. My eyes went unfocused. I tried to make sense of it. Rixon's father, bleeding out. Rixon's knife protruding from his leg—the same knife I'd used to cut Ms into the tunnel walls. Rixon finding me down here, when his father told me he never would.

A picture crystallized in my mind.

But it was the other things he'd said—things about the portal, about the blackness deep—that had my stomach twisting.

Somewhere beneath the palace was a portal to hell. And somewhere beyond that portal was the blackness deep.

And that blackness deep? It wanted to get out. Goosebumps spread over my skin. I shivered. I'd felt it, the pressure, the power. I'd seen the murals—understood them for what they were. A warning, a foreshadowing, perhaps even a possibility that history might repeat itself.

I'd also seen the blood. I'd seen the way the king never removed his gloves. Seen his bandaged hand as he lay there on the floor, dying. I'd seen the long gash on Rixon's palm, too. A childhood wound he couldn't remember.

And then there'd been the king's obsessive need to find Rixon —his son and heir—and keep him close to home. His need to place him on the throne, when other bastards would do. That need was driven by more than just selfish desire.

One by one, pieces fell into place. Pieces I didn't want fitting together. As if to spite me, they clicked, shifting and settling into permanency. I had a picture I didn't want to consider.

"No..." I whispered, blinking, not quite seeing the rest of my cell. My hands unconsciously fussed with the Nebrine shackles at my wrists, pulling, rubbing the raw places where they chaffed. *This* was why Rixon needed to keep him alive.

We needed answers.

I sat with these questions, my mind swirling, for hours. At some point, one of the king's guards, whom I'd seen outside his chambers, came down bearing a plate of food. "What happened with the king?" I demanded.

He merely pressed his lips into a tight line, then walked off. I made a dangerous noise in the back of my throat, frustration and unease warring inside me. Finally, I picked up my plate and took it to the table, picking at the bread and cheese, tasting none of it.

I'd sensed this. Somehow, as we'd crested the hill and first laid eyes on Corinna. I'd sensed something about the city that would change things. And yet, I'd been stupid, naive enough to believe we could escape unscathed—

"Mina."

"Rixon!" I gasped, jumping to my feet, whirling to face him. "You—" I stopped short and took him in. Rumpled, bloodied clothing, messy hair, hands hanging limp at his sides, one of them grasping the king's crown. His throat bobbed. "What happened?" I whispered, rushing to him. I tried to reach through the bars, but my shackles wouldn't allow it.

All I wanted was to comfort him, to wrap my body around him, to kiss away the bleak expression off his face. There were lines, deep grooves of exhaustion I had never seen him wear. He blinked, as if coming around, then dropped the crown and stretched his blood-stained arms through the bars, reaching for me. I moved forward, let him pull us together, sighing. I was trembling, I realized. Exhausted, emotional...*scared*. We hugged, a barrier of *Nebrine* between us.

"I..." His voice was a croak. "I needed to see you."

"What happened?" I whispered, wanting to stay in his arms.

"I cannot find the key," he said. "I asked the guards. I...you're stuck in this fucking cell when I need you. I'll keep looking."

His voice was an angry growl. "Until then, you're leashed, until I can get you out, and get those damned shackles—"

"Rixon! What *happened*?" I pulled away, to better see him, frowning at what was there.

His mouth opened and closed. Then his throat bobbed. "My father. He's..." He took a deep breath, his expression hardening. Then he squared his shoulders and stepped away, as if preparing to deliver a proclamation I wasn't going to like.

Somehow, I already knew what was coming.

"The king is dead," he said. "Mina, I...I gave him my word. The crown has passed to me, and I have accepted. Raeria has a new king. It's me."

My world crumbled from beneath my feet.

Epilogue

The demon prince hovered in the sky high above Corinna's palace, pulling its awareness back into itself. It was over—the king was dead. Now, the demon felt nothing but resignation. The last line of Kozma was all that stood between the barrier keeping hell at bay.

Unless a new heir was born.

Even then, the solution would be temporary, as it always had been. The demon prince had tried to warn them, long ago. Had the world listened? Of course not. Listen to a demon? Such a notion was preposterous. Instead, they'd chosen the easy way out.

Perhaps now, they would pay the price.

The demon had always known history would repeat itself. Once more, hell would suffer for it. The prince loved its kingdom with fierce, unending pride. Yes, hell was dark. Yes, the beings within were capable of great violence and destruction, but only when presented with a world such as this.

The demon's mind turned towards the one person who might fix this. The witch...she was different. Something in her called to its people. Something about her made it wonder, *perhaps this time things will be different.*

Was it too much to hope?

The demon prince sighed, giving the capital city one final look then turned inland with a flap of its wings.

ACKNOWLEDGMENTS

Embarking on a new set of Lady Witch books was intimidating as hell. The first trilogy felt straightforward because it fell within the structure of a love story. As I began planning the second trilogy, I realized that I needed to shift gears. I needed to dive deeper into the demon aspect, world politics, and the witches of the Citadel. I even needed to give Mina a bit of a downfall arc (oh the horror!). Hence, this book took a lot more effort than the others. I anticipate the next two will be even more challenging.

I have Ania Calka to thank for a crucial part of my plot development. We had multiple calls where I word vomited plot ideas, went off on tangents, and somehow she managed to follow everything. She even helped me arrive at an ending that I had not initially imagined. So, thank you, Ania.

A big thanks to my husband, too. He keeps his complaints to a minimum when I lock myself away for days on end during the drafting process. He's always so supportive.

To Jeanine Croft, for her beautiful cover design. I always fall more and more in love with each one. Thank you for always wow'ing me.

A special thanks to some additional valuable people who helped me fine tune everything during the editing process:

Ania Calka, Elianna Lucas, Katarina Vertin, Katrina Cozens, Carina Scherbel, and Anastasia Rivera. There's no such thing as working an a vacuum when you're an author. You ladies are amazing, seriously! Thank you.

Finally, to you the reader, for loving the initial trilogy enough to step into the next leg of Mina and Rixon's journey. I couldn't do it without you. Many heartfelt thanks. See you for the next one!

About the Author

Physics Ph.D by day, author by night, Melissa Mitchell is best known for her ongoing Dragonwall Series. She discovered her love of writing during the final stages of her Ph.D program. She began publishing independently in 2018 after years on Wattpad and numerous pleas for physical copies. Currently, she resides with her husband and dog in Atlanta, Georgia where she works as an optical engineer. When she's not writing, you can find her buried in a book. Besides reading and writing, she enjoys other hobbies like bullet journaling, figure skating, playing piano, and baking cookies.

Visit her online at: authormelissamitchell.com

instagram.com/melissa.nicole.mitchell